Famous'

Destiny

The Monster In The Forest

Alexis Anicque

Just in case you missed it Finding Famous was the beginning of the Famous adventures. You can order an autographed copy directly from the author.

AlexisAnicque.com

This book is dedicated to my beautiful and amazing daughter Kayla Rizzo. Without her this story would never have happened. After reading Finding Famous, she insisted on knowing what happened to the monster in the forest. So, I wrote this book specially for her. She's a **caring Mom and a brilliant teacher**. I'm extremely grateful for her doing the final edit. I'm truly blessed because she amazes me every day.

I am beyond grateful for all of the love, help, and support from my husband Vincent Rizzo, my dear friends Carl and Leslie Hauquitz, and my brother and sister in law, Scott and Dorene Robison. I cannot possibly say how challenging editing is so I must give great thanks to Gordon Krull for his help with editing.

Famous' Destiny

The Monster In The Forest

CONTENTS:

PROLOGUE

After the death of her mother—the time of the great sadness—Famous was alone and searching for answers. The day had finally come to face her fears and deal with the realities of moving on. Magically, her mother had spoken to her from her journal about the journey she had taken to find Famous—a journey Famous would also take.

A journey that led her to the forest where the wizard (of sorts) lived. A journey to find herself, the path her mother had taken so many years before to find her. An adventure through the forest to the waterfall. Trekking to the sea, a ship across the ocean to the castle of a beautiful princess.

This princess was the key to Famous finding Famous. One key and only a part of the truth to where she came from and who she was. This princess was cursed to live all of eternity as a prisoner. Her mother had tried to help, but it was Famous who was to break the spell and lift the curse.

Once the curse was lifted Famous' adventures continue on to Famous' Destiny.

CHAPTER ONE

Is Anyone There?

And just like that the spell was broken and the curse was lifted. The bright light had disappeared, and her world had gone dark. Famous was alone in the darkness. "Hello, is anyone there?" No one answered. Again, she called out—again and again and yet still no answer. Famous sat in the darkness trying to make sense of what happened. She replayed the whole thing in her mind: laying out the amulets, breaking the spell, removing the curse… and darkness.

"Well, I can't just sit here in the dark." Her voice echoed which gave her an eerie feeling. Her voice trembled slightly, "Hello?" She wasn't sure if she should be terrified that she seemed to be alone or be grateful. Then another thought crossed her mind, which was much worse: What if she wasn't alone?

She needed to take some kind of action and find a light or a door. Crawling seemed to be the safest bet. While she crawled along the floor, her fingertips brushed a coin. *No,* she thought, *an amulet.* One of seven, she picked it up and shoved it into her pocket as she continued to crawl, occasionally calling out in the darkness.

It was pitch black. "The complete absence of light," she said. Her words echoed in the room again. Her heart rate jumped, and she felt a slight warmth from her pocket as she crawled along feeling for the other amulets.

"Faaaamous." In the darkness she thought she heard her name. It was spooky and sounded drawn out like they pronounced every syllable. Was she being taunted?

"Helloooo?!" she called out again with a little more panic in her voice. "Is anyone there?" She found another amulet and tried to visualize what the room looked like before the lights went out. It had been such a long, horrible day. Her stress level was beginning to skyrocket.

The more she concentrated on the events that led her to this moment, the warmer the amulet felt in her pocket. Her hand and pocket began to glow. She reached into her pocket, pulled out the first amulet, and examine both amulets at one time. The amulets were slightly glowing in her hand. Famous lifted her hand to see her surroundings and the light started to dim.

As the light faded back to darkness, she started to become more afraid. "Okay, Famous think. Calm down and think!" She could hear her voice. It seemed so loud. She continued to crawl along until she ran into a wall—headfirst, of course. She rubbed her head where it had bumped into the wall. She began feeling the wall as she rose from the floor. She decided it would be best to walk, feeling along the wall searching for the door. She brushed her hand along the wall to a corner and continued to the next corner and the next and so on—until she had made it to a fifth corner.

Her heart began thumping, "Rooms don't normally have five corners so I'm back where I started and no door." No door. The words repeated in her head again: *no door*!

Suddenly she heard a scratching noise from the other side of the room. She jumped back against the wall, "Who's there?" No answer. She couldn't help thinking of rats or rabid dogs like in all of those thriller movies she'd watched.

Suddenly, she heard a pounding noise. Then, more scratching. The more noise she heard, the harder her heart pounded.

"Famooouuusss." She heard her name again. It terrified her. The voice sounded muffled, or ghostly even.

The two amulets began to feel warm again and started to glow bright enough to dimly light the room. She held her hand out and the light from the amulets began to fade. She stared at them as they went dark. All she could see was blackness dotted by visions of little yellow spots. "I have to find the rest of these."

She crawled across the floor feeling for the amulets. "I'll never find them this way." More scratching and banging, and then she thought she heard muffled voices from the other side of the room again. "Great more scary voices in the walls." She sat up and slowly backed away until she hit the wall. "Hello?" Her voice was shaky and sounded strained.

She sat and tried to reason what was happening. "What if I took Angelica's curse and it bounced back to me and I'm trapped in here for all of eternity?" Her mind started working on overdrive. She felt the cold of the wall on her back as tears began to well up in her eyes. "I have to get out of here." Suddenly the amulets began to get warm again.

"I have to focus. C'mon Famous. Focus." She squeezed the amulets and closed her eyes thinking of the brightest light she could ever imagine. When she opened her eyes, the amulets were glowing. Holding her hand high, she continued to focus her energy on the light. "Four walls, no door. Four walls, no door!" she repeated. Fear raced through her. "Four walls, no door!"

Five small round dots on the floor caught her eye. *The amulets*, she thought. She quickly walked to them and gathered the remaining five amulets. She could swear she heard her name yet again. She held the amulets high, concentrating on light. Heat and light radiated from her hand. They felt like they could burn a hole in her hand.

More banging, more scratching, more voices. She turned to the direction of the noise. There was nothing but a wall. "Famous!" she heard, but couldn't believe her ears. It sounded like Ellie. She walked toward the wall and placed her ear against the wall.

"Ellie?" Famous called out. "Ellie, is that you? Ellie, are you there? Please tell me it's you!"

"Famous? I can hear you. Famous, are you okay?" Ellie replied.

"There's no door, Ellie. I'm trapped!" She was screaming and tears were streaming down her face. "I can't get out! Do you hear me? I can't get out!"

CHAPTER TWO

WHERE'S FAMOUS?

The bright light had dissipated, and everything had gone dark. Angelica was gone, but so was Famous. Ellie glanced around the castle dimly lit by the moonlight shining in from the door. As her eyes focused, somehow, it looked different. "Famous?" she called out, but there was not a reply. She glanced back at Jonathon. "Where's Famous?"

"I don't know she was just here," Jonathon answered. He looked around the room. "Edmond?"

Edmond poked his head in the door. "Over here. I was waiting outside when the door flew open and everything went dark." He joined Ellie and Jonathon. "Where's Famous?"

Ellie walked into the kitchen and back out again. "Not in there. This room looks different to me. Does it look different to you Jonathon?"

"Geez, Ellie, it's been a long time since I've been here. I don't know. I can't remember."

Ellie walked over and placed her hand on the wall. "It's like I just don't remember this wall being here." She traced her hand down the wall around the corner to the doorway leading into the next room. They walked into the next room. "That's odd. There appears to be a room here that was here before." She tapped the wall. "It's right here, but there's no door."

Jonathon walked the length of the wall. He started in one room, then moved to the next and the next. The walls looked the same as all the others. "How can there be a room with no door?" He looked at Edmond and Ellie. "It just doesn't make sense."

Edmond looked around. "Maybe it's outside?" He shrugged and knew it sounded ridiculous, but it was at least an idea.

Ellie paced back and forth. "Famous wouldn't have left on her own. Did either of you see where Daniel went?"

Edmond shook his head, "I was outside. The door flew open and out went the lights."

"Yeah, it all happened so fast!" Jonathon exclaimed.

"Well we have to find her," said Ellie. She became frantic and called for Famous several times.

"Maybe I should go check our place, Ellie. She could have gone back there," reasoned Edmond.

Jonathon shook his head. "I think one of us would have seen her come out the door."

"Hello? Is anybody there?" The voice was muffled.

"Shh. Did you hear that?" Ellie leaned over toward the wall. "Famooouuuuus?" she called out. "I swear I heard her. Did you hear it?"

They shook their heads. "Where was it coming from?" Jonathon asked.

Ellie pointed at the wall. "In there." She put her head to the wall. Jonathon and Edmond did the same.

"Hello?"

"She's in there. We have to find a door!" yelled Ellie.

"Where's the flashlight?" Jonathon asked Edmond.

"I dropped it when the door flew open." He walked outside, but it was dark. The moon had gone behind the clouds. He crouched down and felt along the ground. The grass was damp, and he could feel the cold seeping into the knees of his pants. Edmond stood up. "I can't find it. It's too dark."

"Edmond, can you run to your place and get another one? Oh, and maybe a hammer!" Jonathon shouted from inside. "I'll walk the perimeter of the outside just in case there is a door on the outer wall. Ellie, you stay here and listen for Famous."

"I'm on it," said Edmond, and he took off toward home. At the same time, Ellie nodded and placed her ear back on the wall. She watched as Jonathon disappeared out the door. "Famous," she called out again, but nothing. "Faaamous!"

It seemed like an eternity before Jonathon came back in the door. "I didn't find any door that led to that room, just one off the kitchen," he said.

Edmond came in holding a toolbox and a flashlight. He clicked it on and shone the light along the length of the wall.

"C'mon, Famous. Focus!" Famous yelled. This time, they all heard her yelling from the other side of the wall.

"She's definitely in there!" Edmond exclaimed and he pulled out the hammer and a chisel. "Maybe we can use these and break a hole in the wall." He scraped at the wall with the chisel, then banged on the wall with the hammer. "It's solid as a rock!" They all took turns banging on the wall.

"Jonathon, how is this possible?" Ellie asked.

"Maybe the curse. Maybe Daniel. Maybe…" Jonathon's voice trailed off. "Where is Daniel? He seemed to disappear as soon as Famous said the words." He looked around again and shook his head. "None of this makes sense."

"We have to let her know we are here," Ellie said and she screamed out Famous' name once again.

"Ellie?" Famous called out. "Ellie, is that you?"

Famous? I can hear you. Famous, are you okay?"

"There's no door, Ellie. I'm trapped!" Famous was screaming and tears were streaming down her face. "I can't get out! Do you hear me? I can't get out!"

"I hear you," Ellie replied. She could hear the panic in Famous's voice. "We have to come up with something guys. She looked at the wall. "Famous, what's in there?"

"Nothing. There is nothing, just nothing!" Famous sounded anxious. "Just me. I'm all that's in here!"

Jonathon spoke to her, "Famous, we'll figure this out, but you have to be calm. Do you remember what happened? Did you see Daniel?"

"I...I...don't know. Everything went dark and then I was alone." Alone. The word rang out in her head and tears welled up in her eyes again.

Jonathon looked at Ellie and shrugged. He looked like he was trying to come up with an idea. Finally, one came to him. "Do you have the amulets?" Jonathon asked Famous.

"Yes, I have them."

"Okay good." He looked at Ellie. "Maybe she can use them to get herself out," he told her.

"It's worth a try," Ellie answered.

"I can't hear you. What did you say?" Famous screamed through the wall.

Ellie looked at Jonathon. "Well, whatever you have in mind, you better let her know because she sounds panicky!"

"Famous, you have the power. You must use the amulets to get yourself out," Jonathon shouted.

Famous was sobbing. "I don't know how! Why did this happen Jonathon?" she cried.

"I don't know. Maybe Daniel. Maybe the curse…" He stopped himself, but not in time.

Famous was banging on the wall. "Get me out of here! I don't want to be trapped in here for eternity! Get me out of here! Break down the wall! Please help me!" she screamed, crying and pleading for help.

"Famous, you have to calm down!" Jonathon's words sounded harsher than he meant them to. "Listen, you have the amulets. Use them."

"I don't know the words," Famous whined.

"You don't need words. You are not trying to break a spell. Famous, you need to focus your energy. Visualize a door. Create a door. You can do this! Close your eyes, see the door, and believe it is there."

"I'll try." Famous closed her eyes and squeezed her hands closed tightly around the amulets. It was like holding fire. Her heart pounded so hard she heard it in her ears. The ground started to shake, and the wall rumbled. The sound continued to grow louder and louder.

Ellie felt the ground quake and looked nervously at Jonathon. He placed his hand on her shoulder as the wall began to crack.

"You're doing great! Keep focusing your energy!" Jonathon encouraged Famous.

The wall cracked more and more. Finally, Ellie could see Famous. Ellie caught her breath. Jonathon motioned her to be still.

A portion of the wall crumbled and Famous fainted. It was enough for Ellie to climb in. "Help me get her out of here!" she yelled. Edmond and Johnathon pulled Famous through the crack in the wall. Ellie climbed out and looked Famous over. "She's breathing and doesn't look hurt. Let's get her home."

Jonathon picked Famous up and carried her to Ellie's house. "The stairwell is too narrow to carry her up," he said. He placed her on a large bean bag in the bean bag room. "Famous?" Jonathon repeated her name, trying to wake her. "She's out! Her pulse seems fine. What should we do? She probably just needs rest, right?"

Ellie hovered over them and spoke with concern. "Yeah, I don't know. Should we call a doctor?" she asked. They all stood there staring at her. Suddenly, her eyes fluttered open. "Famous? Are you okay?" Ellie asked.

"I'm just so tired," Famous croaked. She rolled over on to her side and fell asleep.

Ellie brushed her hair back off her face. "I think she's okay. Let's let her sleep."

CHAPTER THREE

THE NEXT MORNING

Famous awoke and rolled off the bean bag. Her body ached like it never had before. She stood up and looked around. It took her a full minute to realize where she was: in the bean bag room at Ellie and Edmond's house. She had no idea how she had gotten there but was grateful just the same. The room glowed softly from the fire in the fireplace. This had been her mom's favorite room. The wall was lined with bookshelves filled with books from all over the world.

Ellie and Edmond's place had once been a castle that they bought and turned into a bed and breakfast. Famous's mother had met them years before and stayed with them on her journey to find Famous. But that's another story.

A noise from the kitchen made her turn around. She slowly tiptoed out of the room and into the foyer, toward the kitchen. Peeking around the corner, she saw Ellie pouring a cup of coffee.

Famous walked around the corner. "I'll take a cup." Ellie jumped and spilled the coffee on the counter. "I'm so sorry. I didn't mean to scare you."

Ellie set the pot down, ran to Famous, and threw her arms around her. "It's okay," she said. "I'm so glad to see you." Famous grimaced in pain. "Are you okay?"

"I think so, for the most part. I do hurt everywhere."

"It was a rough night. Actually, it's been a couple of rough weeks."

Ellie walked back over to the counter and poured fresh cups of coffee for herself and Famous. They sat down at the table.

Famous stirred sugar in her coffee and stared in the cup as the liquid swirled. "Now what?" Famous looked lost. "I mean, I can't go back, can I?"

Ellie touched her hand. "I think you need to just take a minute. Take some time to digest what's happened. You know, time to figure this out. You've had quite a shock!"

"Good morning." Famous and Ellie's heads turned to see Jonathon. "I hope I didn't startle you. How are you feeling this morning Famous?"

"Tired, achy, and a little confused," Famous groaned.

"I bet! That was some night, wasn't it? But you know the one thing I don't understand? Where did Daniel go?" He poured himself a cup of coffee and refilled the women's cups. Jonathon joined them at the table.

"Really?" asked Famous. "What about where did my grandmother go? Why was I imprisoned in a room with no door? Not even to mention in a room that didn't exist yesterday morning. Well, one of the walls didn't, anyway. I can actually think of a bunch of other things I completely don't understand."

Jonathon nodded in agreement. "I am just saying all the things he had done to get those amulets and poof! He's just gone. Just like that. It seems too easy and somewhat suspicious to me."

Ellie stood up and walked in the kitchen. "Well, one thing I am sure of is that no one is confused about hunger. How about I whip up some breakfast?"

Jonathon gulped the last of his coffee. "Wish I could stay, but I have to get back to teach a class."

"I feel like I need to keep myself busy," said Famous. "I have so much to think about. I would love to help you with breakfast, Ellie." Famous stood up from the table as Edmond came into the room. "Good morning Edmond. Ellie and I are going to fix up some breakfast. Are you hungry?"

"Definitely, so how did everyone sleep last night?" Edmond asked.

Famous responded with a yawn and poured a cup of coffee for Edmond. She started pulling food from the fridge. Ellie followed her lead and took pans from the cupboard. Famous began mixing batter for muffins. She thought back to her time with her mother. She added a dash of nutmeg, a little cinnamon, and some orange zest.

"Ellie, I'm thinking scrambled eggs with cheddar. Maybe some sliced tomatoes, bacon, and muffins with icing on the side. What do you think?" Famous asked.

It was a pretty fancy breakfast with no guests there, but Ellie was sure Famous needed it to distract her thoughts. She remembered when Famous's mother, Dar, was alive. They baked and cooked together all the time.

"El…?"

"Oh, sorry, yeah. That sounds great Famous. I guess I was lost in thought."

"No problem, I get it." Famous set confectioners' sugar in front of Ellie. "Do you want to make the icing?"

"Sure thing," Ellie answered as she grabbed a whisk and a bowl.

Edmond came into the kitchen. "Wow, looks like quite a feast for just the three of us," he remarked.

Famous smiled. "Is it too much?" shed asked.

"No way. Literally my favorite part of having guests is I get a big breakfast." He refilled his cup of coffee. "Anything I can do to help?"

Famous handed him plates and silverware. "You could set the table."

Jonathon came back in the dining area from the stairs carrying his travel bag. "I thought I'd say goodbye and let you know I'll try to make it back this evening, but I wouldn't count on it." They all said their good-byes to Jonathon and Famous walked him to the door. "Famous, I hope to talk to you soon about the last few days." She smiled, nodded, and watched him walk to his car.

Famous returned to the kitchen. Ellie pulled the muffins from the oven to cool while Famous cooked the bacon and sliced the tomatoes. Edmond set the table. The room was quiet, each of them lost in their own thoughts.

As Famous carried over the plates of tomatoes and bacon and bowl of scrambled eggs on the table, she thought the massive table that was normally set for ten looked mostly empty. She carefully set them down and Ellie followed her with the plate of freshly iced muffins. Everyone took their seats.

"Famous, this looks great," marveled Ellie as she began dishing food onto her plate. "So, Edmond, what is on your agenda for the day?"

"The usual: cut and stack firewood. I do have to go into town and get some supplies. So, if you need anything, I can pick it up. I know we have guests coming in the next few days," he replied.

"I'll help get the rooms ready for you, Ellie," Famous chimed in.

"It sounds like I can take the day off," Ellie laughed.

They ate their breakfasts and continued chatting about their plans for the day. After they finished and the kitchen was clean, Edmond left and Famous busied herself helping Ellie with the daily tasks—cleaning rooms, washing linens, vacuuming, and such.

Ellie brought Famous a letter that had been hand delivered for her. It was just a plain white envelope with *Famous* written on it. She placed the envelope in her apron and immediately noticed heat radiating from it.

Famous walked in the bean bag room intending to read whatever was in the envelope in private. Walking along, she ran her hand down the shelves of books. She stopped at a book that seemed to call to her. The cover appeared to be worn and had no lettering on the spine. She pulled it from the shelf and opened the cover. "The Mystery of Witches and Magic Spells," she read aloud.

Forgetting about the letter, she sat near the fire in the bean bag that her mother had sat in so many years before. She opened the book and began to read about witches. Soon, her eyes grew heavy and she drifted off to sleep.

Famous slept for hours. She wasn't sure if she was awake or still dreaming when she felt a small ball of fur cuddle her side. Surely, she was dreaming. A moment later she felt another furry little critter snuggling into the curve of her back. Her eyes fluttered as she remembered back to the cottage in the forest. It seemed so long ago. *Certainly*, she thought, *I must be dreaming*. But she knew she was awake when the third wrapped itself around her neck.

She opened her eyes. "What are you doing here?" She scratched their little heads and petted the creatures. "Is Jeremiah here?" She asked.

CHAPTER FOUR

YOU ARE REALLY HERE!

Ellie tiptoed out of the bean bag room when she found Famous sleeping. She was glad to see her getting some much-needed rest. A knock on the door startled her as she glanced back to see Famous was still sleeping. She sprinted to answer the door before they knocked again. A small chubby man who reminded her of Santa stood at the door.

"Hello, can I help you with something?" Ellie asked.

The man chuckled. "I'm sorry I didn't call first. I am Jeremiah. I'm here to see Famous." Ellie stared at him thinking he looked exactly how Dar and Famous had described him. "You see, I only had the address from the letters she sent. I had no phone number or any other information. Otherwise, I would have called first. May I come in?"

Ellie opened the door wider. "Oh my, yes, of course. Let me help you with your bag." She picked up the case and noticed it had netting along each side and something moved inside. "Is this a dog or a cat?"

"Neither actually, but they are quite well behaved. Do you mind if I let them out? I promise they'll not cause problems or leave a mess. They have been cooped up for some time."

"Absolutely. Please, come in and let them out. Famous is sleeping and I'd rather not wake her. I was getting ready to start working on dinner ideas. How about some tea or coffee? Would you like to keep me company in the kitchen?"

"Where's the kitchen? I'd be happy to help with dinner, tea sounds great. Famous wrote me a week or so ago, I have been very worried about her." Jeremiah opened the bag and three little furballs scurried out and immediately ran off to find a good hiding spot. "They'll be fine now." He ignored her startled look as she watched them scurry away. She remembered Famous telling her stories about furry little creatures but figured she had been dreaming. They walked into the kitchen.

Ellie started a kettle of water and pulled out some peppermint tea. "Is that why you came all this way? Because you were worried."

Jeremiah sat at the table and watched Ellie busy about the kitchen. "Um, no, not exactly. It's urgent…"

Edmond walked in. "Hello, honey," he said and kissed her on the cheek. He glanced at Jeremiah. "Who is this?"

She smiled. "Jeremiah!"

"Jeremiah, as in the-cottage-in-the-forest, Jeremiah?" he asked.

"That's me!" Jeremiah responded. He stood up and shook Edmond's hand. "I've come to see Famous, but since she is sleeping, I am going to help Ellie with dinner. Oh, but before that I just realized I should have asked if you have any rooms available because if not, I should probably call and get a room in town before it gets too late."

Ellie turned to Edmond. "We can put him in the orange room next to Famous. There are no bookings on that room for the week, I'll just block it off on the site."

"Great,! Where are your bags? I'll take them up and show you around a bit," Edmond offered.

Ellie reminded herself of the bag full of strange animals. "I didn't notice any bags other than…"

"Don't worry about my bags," Jeremiah chuckled. "You see, I… um… well, it's hard to explain. Let's just say I travel light."

Edmond led Jeremiah up the narrow winding staircase.

"This is the yellow room where Famous is staying," Edmond explained. "Here, right next door, is the orange room." He opened the door for Jeremiah. The room was brilliantly decorated with orange floral arrangements. "I hope it's not too girly for you."

"It's quite lovely, I'm so happy that you have something available."

Edmond opened the curtains. "It's slow this time of year." Then, he opened the closet. "Here is the closet… not that you need it."

While his back was turned Jeremiah took his bag from his pocket and placed it on the bed. With a wave of his hand, it grew into a much larger bag.

Edmond turned to see the large bag on the bed. "That's strange I didn't notice you having that bag."

"I've had it with me the whole time." Jeremiah smiled, his eyes twinkling.

Edmond shrugged it off and gave Jeremiah a quick tour of the upstairs.

"So, what brought you to Ireland?" Edmond asked as they walked back down the stairs.

"It's imperative that I—"

"Did you get him all settled?" Ellie interrupted.

"Yes ma'am. Now how about we get started on that dinner?" Jeremiah replied and went in the kitchen. He moved about like he had cooked there many times before. "How about spaghetti? It's pretty easy to whip up."

"Sounds divine," Ellie grinned. "I'll make a salad. Edmond, looks like you get to set the table again."

Edmond grabbed four plates and turned to Ellie. "Is Jonathon coming back for dinner? Is anyone else going to be here for dinner?"

"Hmm, you know, I don't think so. We actually don't have any guests staying tonight and if Jonathon shows up, we can grab another plate."

"You are really here! I thought I was dreaming," exclaimed Famous. The three of them turned when they heard her voice. Famous hugged Jeremiah so tight it hurt, but she didn't care. "I can't believe you're here. I thought you never left the forest."

Jeremiah chuckled and hugged her tight. "Yes, I am really here, and right now, I am helping Ellie with dinner."

As Jeremiah and Ellie brought the food to the table, Famous asked, "Jeremiah?"

"Hmm?"

"I'm so happy you're here, but I'm also wondering why you came all this way."

He smiled. "To see you, of course."

"And that's all there is to it?" She didn't sound convinced.

"I'm really tired from such a long journey. Let's just enjoy dinner and we can talk about it more later." They sat at the table and Jeremiah began by passing the spaghetti around. They then took turns passing the salad and the garlic bread.

Famous could feel heat coming from the letter in her pocket. She had forgotten all about it. She tried to push the thought from her head. "Ellie, doesn't it seem so strange having so few people at the table? You were busier last week, huh, Ellie?" Famous inquired.

"We have more guests coming tomorrow," Ellie responded. "It's been a little bit slow lately. With all that's been going on, I guess it's a good thing." Ellie took another bite.

"It *has* been a dreadful couple of days," Famous said dramatically. "I have been to Russia and back, got kidnapped, had to break a spell to lift a curse, and got trapped in a dark room with no door."

"You will have to tell me all about it. It sounds quite exciting," said Jeremiah. They continued small talk for a while.

Famous took one more bite from her garlic bread and let out a big sigh. "This is really delicious, you two really outdid yourselves. I'm nearly stuffed and yet, I keep eating."

They emptied their plates, then sat at the table telling Jeremiah the story about Angelica, all the rest of the places Famous had gone, and, of course, about Daniel.

"And you have no clue where Daniel went?" Jeremiah asked.

"No, but I'm sure I'm not rid of him for good. Especially because I have the seven amulets. I am going to have to figure out what I'm going to do next."

Had Famous not been looking at Jeremiah, she may have missed the suddenly serious look on his face before it disappeared. She started to ask him what was going on, but Ellie got up to clean the table. Famous got up and began to help clearing the dishes from the table.

"I'll get the dishes," Edmond announced as he went in the kitchen and began to run water to fill the sink. "It's the least I can do after a meal like that."

Jeremiah got up and took his dish to Edmond. "Thank you. I'm feeling quite exhausted. I think I'll turn in."

Famous stood up. "But I was hoping we could talk more."

Jeremiah wrapped his arm around Famous. "We do have a lot to talk about, but it's probably best with a clear head." He hugged her tight, said good night, and went up the winding stairs to his room.

CHAPTER FIVE

THE SUMMONING

Famous ached as she climbed the stairs. She was tired and longed for a good night sleep. Thoughts of Jeremiah traveling all the way to Ireland crept into her mind. There had to be something more to it. He wasn't the kind to just leave the forest and show up for a visit unannounced. Now that she thought of it, he wasn't the kind to leave the forest at all.

As she reached the top of the stairs, she could see a glowing light coming from under her door. Thoughts of Daniel came to her mind. Famous looked back at the stairs and then to the door to the room where she knew Jeremiah was surely sleeping. Heat radiated from the letter in her pocket.

She stood there frozen in an internal debate. Should she run down the stairs, wake Jeremiah, or just open the door? Famous slowly tip-toed to her room door and placed her ear on the door to listen, but there was no sound. There was a bright green glow coming from her room. She watched to see a shadow of movement or a change in the light, but she saw neither. She again pressed her ear firmly against the door, but still, no sound came from the other side. She reached for the doorknob and slowly turned. *Here goes*, she thought. Her heart was pounding as she began to push the door open, the door creaking loudly as she opened it up wide. The glow was coming from a book lying on her bed. As she got closer to the bed, she realized it was one of her mother's journals. It had never done that before.

Famous remembered that her mother had said things would become clear and words had appeared in the journal. She knew there must have been something magical about the journals, but to what extent was completely unclear to her. She opened the journal and began to read.

Today I made the decision it was time for me to take Famous home to New York. I received a letter from her birth grandmother. She wanted to see Famous, so I met with her today. I had so many questions. She told me the story of the summoning.

The story began many years before. Hundreds of years of white witches correcting the evils of curse-casting witches. Famous's birth mother, Destiny, had a book written many years ago. It was a way to undo a spell— an evil curse that had been put on a beautiful princess who had stolen seven amulets from an evil witch's house. Each amulet was placed in different locations until the death of the curse-caster. Destiny added the locations of each amulet to the book in the form of a riddle.

Upon the death of the evil witch, a pure one's child would be able to break the curse and end the evil witch's spell forever. Her child would be the one, one of a small number of descendants that could break the curse. She knew it would be years before her child could understand. She would take her child and the amulets and together, break the curse.

Everything had been written in the book, but she had taken ill nearing the end of her pregnancy. She had placed the book in the hands of a librarian to keep safe for her. Before dying in childbirth, she told her mother where she had to take the last amulet and her child. Destiny's mother, Angelica, ached over losing her daughter. Now she knew she would have to give up her granddaughter as well. She had to find a mother for her granddaughter. Someone kind and loving that would lead her back to the family when it was safe.

Angelica spent a week summoning her family and the community of white witches. They came from faraway places, traveled for days to come to Angelica's aid. The baby was only two weeks old when they gathered to cast her fate. The day the witches came together would never be forgotten. They met on the eve of a full moon. Thunder roared, lightning struck, and the earth seemed to stand still. Each witch brought her own sacred medallion, amulet, or other heirloom that had passed through generations and generations. This day was to be a celebration of the baby girl, a day that the witches would cast a spell to find the child a mother.

It was nearing midnight when they placed her in the center of the pentagram. Surrounded by candles, the witches began to chant. Each witch using their powers to summon one of a pure heart to find and be a mother to the girl. They went to her in her dreams. They called her to take a journey to find her baby.

The following day, Angelica began the trek to the monastery. This was the place she was to leave her precious grandchild. The witches continued to summon *the one chosen to be her mother. They would visit her dreams until the day she had her in her loving arms.*

Dar Alegria began having dreams—dreams so real of a child. A child that needed a mother. This baby was to be her child, she was being summoned to find her child. Dar began her journey to find her child. This journey would be the beginning of Famous's Destiny.

Many years later, Famous followed her mother's journal to where she had found Famous. This adventure brought Famous back to her grandmother, Angelica...

The words began to blur, and her eyes grew heavy. Dreams of witches flying on brooms filled her head. Daniel was chasing her through the forest. She was running as fast as she could. It was damp, cold, and dark. Famous was dreaming about the forest, but the trees had eyes and the branches seemed to be trying to grab her. She kept looking back and would see a shadow that she believed was Daniel. A scream escaped her lips and she sat up. It took several seconds for her to realize she was still in her room and she had been dreaming.

Her mother's journal was lying on the floor. The blankets were hanging off the bed and sweat was dripping from her forehead. Famous stepped out of bed and there were leaves all around on the floor. She took another step. The leaves were slightly damp and sticking to her feet. Famous lifted her foot, plucked a leaf off, and rubbed it between her fingers. Stepping closer to the journal, she felt a twig or branch dig deep into her foot. She cringed in pain, grabbed her foot, and sat back on the edge of the bed.

Looking around the room, everything seemed to look the same. It was dark but by all appearances, the walls, the bathroom door, the closet door, and even the armoire were as they had been when she laid down earlier in the evening. Famous looked down at the floor and could see shadows or shapes of leaves everywhere except there seemed to be a small path leading to the door.

Slowly, she stood and crept along the path to the door. She reached for the doorknob, but it seemed to move farther away from her. She reached again and again, each time it seemed to be farther from her reach. The room darkened.

Suddenly, she heard a ghostly whisper. "Famous, where are the amulets?" Famous looked around, but there was no one there. Again, she heard, "Famous, where are the amulets?" She could understand the words but could not recognize the voice because it was only a faint whisper. The whisperer repeated the question only this time pausing after each word in a demanding manner.

"Who's there?" she whispered back, but there was no reply. Famous walked with her arms extended like a mummy in the direction of the door to stop herself from crashing into the door or wall in the darkened room. She continued to feel the leaves sticking to her feet.

She felt the soft fur of one of Jeremiah's creatures brush against her ankle and reached down to pick it up. She held the little creature tightly against her chest and reached for the doorknob. The room began to glow. Nervously, Famous looked behind her and saw that the light was coming from her mother's journal. "Famous, don't be scared, you are safe!" This time, the voice was clear. It sounded like her mother.

Famous turned and walked back to the journal, whispering, "Mom?" As she bent down to pick up the journal it snapped closed. Famous was very confused. She glanced all around, but the room seemed so dark now. Her eyes were filled with yellow spots. She looked back towards the door then back to the journal. The spots slowly disappeared as her eyes readjusted to the darkness.

The fur baby seemed to be getting restless. It jumped from her arms and scurried under the bed. Famous called to it making kissing noises. Then she remembered the lamp on her bedside table. Why she hadn't thought about the lamp next to the bed until this moment she didn't know. She walked along the bed and switched on the lamp. On all four of the walls, written over and over were the words *where are the amulets?*

CHAPTER SIX

DID YOU DO THIS?

Famous gasped and ran to the door. She flung it open, ran to Jeremiah's door, and began to bang on it. "Jeremiah!" she screamed. "Jeremiah!"

Jeremiah opened the door rubbing his eyes, "Famous, what time is it?" The light coming from her room showed the look of panic or terror on her face. "What's wrong? Are you okay?"

She grabbed his hand and nearly dragged him to her room. "I thought I was dreaming, or should I say, having a nightmare. But you have got to see this." They entered her room and as they crossed the threshold Jeremiah paused. He stared at the walls and then the leaves covering the floor. "How is this possible?" she asked with panic in her voice. "Have you ever seen anything like this in your life?"

He was shaking his head and looked to be trying to make sense of it. A noise behind them made them jerk their heads to look back. Ellie and Edmond were standing at the top of the stairs. "Holy cow, what in the world?" Ellie exclaimed as she glanced around the room.

"I don't know! I was reading one of my mother's journals and must have dozed off. I had a nightmare about Daniel chasing me in the forest. I heard voices, whispers, and…" Famous waved her hand through the air. "I don't know. I mean, it doesn't seem possible. How? All these leaves, the writing… I was right here. The whole time, I was here! How is this possible?"

Ellie placed her arm around Famous's shoulder. "I can't think of any way to explain this. Anybody?"

Edmond shook his head. "I've got nothing. Jeremiah?"

"Nope, not a thing."

They stood there just staring for several minutes. "So, I guess I need to rake my room," Famous chuckled trying to make light of the situation. "This seems pretty unreal. It has me wondering if I'm still dreaming."

"Well, if you are, so am I! This is creepy. Let's go downstairs and get you a cup of tea," Ellie sighed. "You can sleep in the bean bag room tonight and tomorrow we'll get this mess cleaned up." Ellie turned Famous by the shoulders and steered her out of the room. She nudged Famous toward the stairs anxiously wanting to get her away from the situation.

"I'm not sure I'll be getting much more sleep tonight. Do you have any more paint in this color?" Famous asked tiredly. "It looks like I'll need to do the whole room."

"Don't worry about it, Famous. I'll take care of it," Edmond answered as he closed the gap between him and Ellie.

"That doesn't seem fair," Famous said as she tromped down the stairs.

Jeremiah took one last look around the room, flipped off the lamp, shut the door, and quickly caught up with the others. One by one they walked down the spiral staircase without saying a word. There were no words that could possibly explain what had happened.

Ellie walked into the kitchen and flipped on the kettle. She retrieved the tea bags and the sugar bowl from the cupboard and placed them on the table. A thought had come to her mind and without thinking, she blurted it out. "Is it just me or does it seem odd that you were dreaming about Daniel chasing you in the forest and now you have the remnants of a forest in your room?" Everyone stopped and stared at Ellie.

Jeremiah spoke up first. "Well, I had thought that very same thing, but there is more to consider."

Famous looked confused. "What do you mean?"

Ellie had gone into the kitchen and came back with four cups. She was setting them on the table and filling each one with hot water. She hadn't heard what Jeremiah had said so she continued her thought. "I'm just wondering if it's possible that you... I mean, that it was so... I don't want you to take this the wrong way, but—"

"Ellie are you thinking that I dreamt my nightmare into reality because I'm a witch?"

Famous interrupted. Famous had said it like she was wondering if it was possible, not like she was accusing Ellie of pointing fingers. "I do still have the amulets in my pocket and I'm still not really sure how this whole amulets and witchy thing works. Hmm, I guess it seems plausible."

Famous had forgotten what Jeremiah had said. She looked to be contemplating the issue as she sipped her tea. Jeremiah cleared his throat. "That does actually sound like a possibility." He emphasized as he said *a possibility*. "Or it could be Daniel trying to get the amulets. One question is, how does that theory work with the words on the walls?"

"I think I'm going to need to get in touch with Jonathon tomorrow," Famous said. "Today, actually. I should go up and get my phone." Famous cringed at the thought and suddenly she felt heat coming from the amulets in her pocket, which reminded her of the letter she had gotten earlier that day. "Ellie do you know who the letter was from that was delivered today?"

"I think it is from your grandmother," answered Ellie

"I had forgotten all about it with Jeremiah showing up. Maybe that will have some answers in it. It's in the pocket of my apron upstairs."

"No one is going back in your room tonight!" Ellie's tone was anxiously stern. "It's just too weird. Besides, we all should get some rest. I can't remember what time the guests will be here tomorrow, but they are paying guests, so I have got to get some rest. Famous, do not even think of going back to your room. We seriously have to figure something out because we can't have episodes like tonight with guests here."

Jeremiah stood up. "I feel like Famous and I should leave and go back to the forest in the morning," he stated.

"What? No. That wasn't what I was saying, Jeremiah. I am happy you are here. I... we don't want either of you to go." Ellie looked at Edmond with tears in her eyes. "Tell them, Edmond."

"Ellie's right. Neither of you should be leaving. We want you here and there is still so many questions," Edmond said.

Famous shook her head. "No. Maybe he's right. This is getting out of control. And who knows how long it will take to answer those questions? I am not willing to jeopardize your safety or your livelihood."

"Listen!" Jeremiah said loudly. "There's a monster in the forest!" They stared at him speechless. "There is a myth, I am not going into it right now, but I need Famous's help. I need her to come back to the forest with me. I know you have a lot going on here, but Famous, you are the only one that can help."

Famous stood up and paced around the room. "What about my dream? This can't be a coincidence. Did you consider that Jeremiah?" Famous walked out of the room, through the foyer and into the bean bag room. She plopped down on her favorite one by the fire. A fur ball curled up on her lap reminding her that she had left one of the others up in her room.

She scrambled up from the bean bag back through the foyer, into the dining area to the staircase. Ellie grabbed her hand. "Famous, where are you going? Just let it go for tonight."

Famous pulled from her grasp. "I can't. Jeremiah, one of the creatures is up in my room. You know you're going to have to give each of them a name. Anyway, I was holding one of them. It jumped down and scurried under the bed. I don't remember seeing it leave the room, so it may be trapped up there." Famous began to climb the stairs. Jeremiah followed.

"I guess I'll go too," Edmond shrugged.

Ellie followed Edmond, loudly muttering to herself, "Fine! If you all are going, why not? I know why not. Because it would probably be just fine if we left it for the last few remaining hours of the night. Truly there are only a few more hours left until daylight. But no. Let's all go upstairs back to the creepiness." She stomped on every step as she continued muttering, "I mean to say that it's probably curled up in a tiny ball sleeping and doesn't have a worry in the world."

She continued to mumble different sarcastic remarks all the way up the stairs but was rendered speechless as they all stood at the doorway staring in the room. The words on the walls were gone, the leaves on the floor were gone, and even the bed was made. It was as if nothing had happened.

"I think this is even creepier than before," Ellie whispered in disbelief. "I know what I saw. Okay, what's everyone thinking now?"

Famous looked back at Ellie, "I'm at a complete loss for words. Jeremiah, what are you thinking?"

"First thought? Haunted castle," he chuckled.

Famous looked at him. "Aren't you supposed to be a wizard of sorts? Wait… did you do this?"

Jeremiah stepped back. "What do you mean, child? I would never do anything to terrify you."

"No, I mean clean it up so I wouldn't feel obligated to stay here and do it? You know, so I would go back to the forest with you. I've seen you do some tricky stuff."

Famous, Edmond, and Ellie stood in the doorway staring at Jeremiah. A little furry face peeked out from under the bed. Jeremiah scooped him up. "There you are, you silly little fur ball." He turned to see them standing there waiting for an answer. "Do you really believe I am capable of that Famous? Besides, I was with you the whole time."

Famous thought back through the night. He hadn't left their presence at all. She was considering it when Ellie pointed out he was the last one out of the room. "Yeah, you turned off the lamp and shut the door," Famous exclaimed in an accusing manner. "A little wave of your hand and a twinkle in your eye and it all disappeared. Is that what happened?"

"I assure you I have no idea what you are talking about," Jeremiah replied indignantly.

Edmond was reminded of the luggage. "Wizard, huh? That would explain the luggage."

Ellie looked at him quizzically. "What luggage? Edmond, what are you talking about?"

"He didn't have luggage and then he did!" Edmond explained.

Famous looked annoyed by Edmonds weird interruption. "Okay, Edmond, you are getting off topic. Jeremiah, did you or did you not make it all disappear?"

"Famous, do you really think he can do that?" Ellie half laughed as she said it. "I think we are all just a little tired and maybe we should get some rest and talk about it further in the morning."

Jeremiah was quick to turn and start for his room. "I agree. Goodnight everyone." He didn't even slow down when Famous started to protest. He was in his room and closing the door before she could get a word out.

"Ellie, really?" Famous scoffed.

"What? It's not like he was going to confess, and I am not sure I would believe it if he did. I'm going downstairs to my room to lay down so I can salvage the last few hours of tonight and get some sleep. You can sleep here or downstairs or whatever you like, but I have to get some sleep." She turned and headed for the stairs. Edmond looked at Famous, shrugged, and followed Ellie downstairs.

"Okay, I can't be the only one freaked out right now. We're talking about this in the morning!" Famous called out, but there was no one there to listen. She sat on her bed to collect her thoughts.

CHAPTER SEVEN

WARNING

Famous was awakened by a knock on the door. The sun was shining brightly through the window curtains. She struggled to open her eyes as she'd only closed them a few hours before. The knock was much louder the second time. "Okay, okay. I'm awake. Come in." No one came in. "Hello, I said come in!" Famous sat up, stepped into her slippers, and stomped to the door. "Really? I said come in!" she practically screeched as she grabbed the doorknob and swung the door open. There was no one there. She looked down the hall in both directions and there was not a soul to be seen.

Famous walked to Jeremiah's door and knocked lightly. There was no answer, so she knocked again a little harder. Still, no answer. She thought about peeking inside but decided not to. She turned to go back to her room and felt a tap on her shoulder. Nervously, she glanced back to the empty hall. "That is not funny!" Quickly, she walked back to her room to change into some jeans and a t-shirt. She pulled the amulets from her pockets from yesterday and put them into her jeans pocket. Famous thought about the previous day and the one before. A short time ago she had a boring normal life—working at the library, reading, and writing as a pastime. She was always longing for an adventure, and now, here she is in Ireland dealing with ghosts, witches, and wizards.

Following the scent of bacon, she found herself walking down the stairs and into the kitchen. The empty room left her wondering where everyone was. At least the coffee was on. She poured herself a cup. It was eerily quiet. Not a sound in the house. She walked through to the bean bag room, then to Ellie's room. The door was open, but her room was empty.

Famous walked through each room upstairs and down. They were all empty. Finally, she decided to check outside as Edmond spent a lot of time chopping wood for the winter. She reached for the doorknob, but the door flew open and knocked her to the floor. The cup of coffee in her hand went flying, spraying hot coffee everywhere. The cup shattered as it hit the wall.

Ellie gasped. "Oh, my goodness! Famous are you okay?" She knelt down beside Famous to check her out.

Edmond put down the armful of logs he was carrying to help. "Famous, I'm so sorry!"

Famous sat there rubbing her forehead and began laughing. "If it's not one thing, it's another. I'm okay." Edmond and Ellie helped her to her feet and guided her to the dining table. "There is coffee everywhere."

"Don't you worry about that we'll get it cleaned up. Let me get you some more coffee." Ellie rushed into the kitchen and got another cup. "Would you like some breakfast?" Ellie could see the lump forming in the center of Famous's forehead. "Are you sure you're okay? You have quite a bump forming on your forehead."

"I'll be fine. I was just trying to find everyone and picked a really bad time to go outside. Where's Jeremiah?"

"I think he's still in bed," Ellie said as she was still hovering over Famous. "Do you feel dizzy?"

"Ellie, seriously. I'm sure that I'm fine. I knocked on Jeremiah's door but he didn't answer."

"Maybe he's still sleeping," Edmond chimed in. "Maybe we should take you to the doctor."

"Why? So I can get my head examined?" Famous laughed. "No thanks. They might decide to commit me. I'm gonna go up and check in on Jeremiah." She began to stand up from her chair.

"Oh no you're not. You just took a good bash to the head. I'll go." Famous sat back down as Ellie stomped toward the stairs.

When Ellie rounded the corner at the top of the stairs, she noticed that Jeremiah's door was open. She walked to the door and peered inside. "Jeremiah are you in here?" She did not see him in the room. "Jeremiah, are you in the bathroom?" Ellie walked to the bathroom door and knocked, but there was no reply. Ellie turned around and Jeremiah was standing right behind her. She grabbed her chest breathing heavily. "You nearly gave me a heart attack! I called out to you, but I didn't see you."

"I was looking out the window at the end of the hall. Sorry I startled you," Jeremiah apologized. "Is Famous up?"

"Yes, she's downstairs. I'm about to fix her some breakfast. Would you like some?" she asked as she moved toward the door.

"Yes, thank you. I can help if you'd like." Jeremiah followed her out of the room. "I like to cook and I'm a pretty good helper in the kitchen." He smiled. "I've got to be getting back to the forest and I am hoping Famous will go with me. I really need her help."

Ellie didn't respond, she just continued her path to the stairs and down to the kitchen.

Once downstairs, Jeremiah greeted everyone. "Good morning!" He caught one glimpse of Famous and rushed over to her. "What on earth happened to you?"

"It was a simple accident. I'm fine."

"You have quite a goose-egg forming. I know just the thing. I have something in my bag." Jeremiah scurried off as quickly as he had come in to retrieve something from his bag.

As Famous waited for Jeremiah, Ellie began pulling out eggs, fruit, and potatoes. "It won't be long. We'll have guests arriving soon," Ellie warned. "I'll make us some breakfast before they get here." She clanked pans as she set them on the stove, lighting burners with matches and checking the bacon that had been warming in the oven. It was quite a sight to watch her work her magic. It was obvious she had grown accustomed to multi-tasking in the kitchen. She looked like a practiced chef.

Edmond had gone to collect the firewood he had left by the door and clean up the coffee mess before anything stained. Jeremiah reappeared with a small satchel that reminded Famous of the leathery doctor bags you see in old movies. "Close your eyes, Famous," he said. "This will only sting a little."

Famous had closed her eyes as she was told. It smelled of cinnamon, orange… maybe lavender, too. As she took in the scents, she suddenly felt an immense heat from the amulets in her pocket. She tried to remember each time that she had felt heat from them. *There must be something…* her mind wandered.

Ellie was peeking from the kitchen. She saw Jeremiah pour liquid on a cloth and place it on Famous's forehead, wave of his hand, and finally attach medical tape to hold the cloth in place. "Oh, Jeremiah I see you have her all doctored up. What did you put on it?" Ellie asked.

"Old remedy. It works wonders," he replied. "She'll be right as rain in no time." Jeremiah's eyes twinkled as he smiled.

"That's great. Would you like to help me with setting the table?"

"Of course." Jeremiah followed her into the kitchen and began taking dishes and condiments to the table.

"I feel ridiculous just sitting here watching you two do all the work. Let me help." Famous started to get up but heard loud protests from the kitchen. She sat back down. "Really. I feel great, like it didn't even happen. My head doesn't even hurt."

Edmond walked in. "Well, I got all the firewood and coffee mess cleaned up. Need any help El?"

"You can help Jeremiah put the food on the table while I get everyone coffee and juice."

Within minutes they had the table filled with food and everyone was sitting down to enjoy the meal together.

"So, should we talk about last night?" Famous asked. She crammed a piece of bacon in her mouth. Each of them looked at her, but not one of them said a word. "Nothing? Well then, I guess we can come back to that. Jeremiah maybe you should tell us about the monster in the forest."

"It's a long story," Jeremiah said. "Actually, more like a fable or a myth. Do you remember that feeling of being followed or chased when you were in the forest, Famous?" Famous nodded. "Well, years and years ago, before I came to live in the forest there was supposedly a mysterious monster. It was said people and animals would go missing, never to be seen again. Only thing is, there is no proof or evidence that anyone has actually gone missing. Only twice since I've lived in the forest has there been anything odd: once when your mother arrived and again when you came to the forest. I'm fairly certain it has something to with you, Famous." Jeremiah sipped his coffee and shoveled a bite of food in his mouth.

"Me?" Famous asked.

"Yes. It started when your mother was on her journey to find you. It seemed to calm down after she left… just strange feelings of being followed. The forest always seemed scarier at night, but then you came and now it's gotten so much worse. When I got your letters about the amulets, I remembered something about them in the old folklore."

Ellie got the pot of coffee and refilled their cups. "But we're so far from there. How could they possibly be the same amulets?" Ellie asked.

Jeremiah was trying to swallow down another bite. "That's what I want to figure out. That's why I am here. I wanted to see them and compare them to the drawings in the book. The way Famous had described them in her letters, they sound identical to the drawings."

"And you're just now mentioning this?" Famous asked as she started to clear the plates from the table, feeling heat stinging her hip from the amulets in her pocket. "In this old book, does it mention anything else about the amulets? You know, like the power they have, or where they—"

A loud knock came from the front door. "Seems too early for the guest to be arriving," Ellie said as she looked at her watch.

Edmond excused himself from the table to check and see who was at the door. He heard another loud knock just before he reached for the doorknob. Hesitantly, he opened the door. A strong gust of wind nearly knocked him over. There was no one there. He glanced around outside only to see a fog appear. It was unclear what he was looking at. Suddenly, the fog dissipated. An eerie cold swept through him. He felt slightly dizzy as he stepped back to close the door.

The amulets were like fire in Famous's pocket. Something was wrong. She could feel it but didn't know what it was. Famous started thinking the heat from the amulets may be warning her. It was the only thing that made sense. But warning her about what?

Edmond looked confused when he came in the room. "I didn't see anyone at the door. But

I can't help feeling like someone or… something, was there."

Jeremiah raised his eyebrow. "It's like the monster in the forest. Do you remember, Famous? That feeling like it was breathing down your neck but looking behind you, there was nothing there."

"I heard a knock this morning. That's what woke me up," Famous admitted. "I said 'Come in' but the door remained closed. The knocking continued until I finally got up and opened the door, and guess what? That's right, there was no one there! We have something going on here. Why do you think that is Jeremiah? I'm wondering if it followed you from the forest and if we need to go back to the forest at all or if, in fact, we actually need to stay here. Last time I tried to leave I ended up back here anyway."

Ellie perked up at the thought of Famous staying. "Well, it's hard to say, but maybe we need to do some research before you make a final decision," Ellie advised.

"Ellie, you have guests arriving and a lot going on. It could be extremely dangerous for us to be here. And disruptive to your guests," Jeremiah countered.

"Jeremiah's got a point, El. If we go, it will surely follow the amulets, or, worse thought, it will follow me." Famous was thinking that her being there was not in the best interests of Edmond and Ellie.

Ellie walked around the table in contemplation. "Possibly, but how do you know they are the same amulets or even if any of this is real? It could all be coincidental or maybe even delusions from lack of sleep. I'm just not sure I am buying into the monster in the forest theory."

"And yet you didn't struggle with the curse on the princess. I think you're just trying to keep us from leaving," Ellie laughed. "So, Jeremiah, where's this folklore book you were talking about?"

"It's upstairs in my room. I'll get it," he answered, then quickly climbed the stairs and walked the short distance to his room. The book was called *The Book of Wisdom*. It was a large, worn leather-bound book with yellowed pages. It told tales of monsters and witches, their origins, and how to get rid of them. Each chapter described in great detail a monster of some kind wreaking havoc and what role witches played as far as spells to create or destroy them. One chapter was solely dedicated to the monster in the forest that Jeremiah so lovingly called home.

Jeremiah retrieved the book from his satchel. He ran his fingers across the lettering on the cover. It was clear to him the words had been burned or branded into the leather. It felt heavy in his hands. He turned to leave the room and was struck hard on the head, rendering him unconscious.

Jeremiah had been gone a long time. Famous began to wonder what was taking him so long. She yelled upstairs, but got no reply. She gave Ellie a worried look and took off up the stairs. Ellie and Edmond were right on her heels. They found Jeremiah laying on the floor. Famous ran to his side and called his name, shaking him. Ellie ran into the bathroom and got a cold washcloth. It took several minutes to bring him back to consciousness.

CHAPTER EIGHT

What Are We Going To Do Now?

"What happened?" Jeremiah asked "We found you unconscious on the floor, you tell us." Famous had placed the cloth on his head. "It looks like you took a hit on the head so don't go trying to get up to fast. Do you remember anything?"

Jeremiah thought for a second. "Well, I had the book… The book! Where's the book?" He sat up and looked around the room. The book was gone.

"How is this possible?" Famous asked. "We were right downstairs. No one else has come or gone. We would have seen them." Famous looked up at Ellie who looked just as scared as she felt.

"How is anything that has happened in the past few days possible?" Ellie replied. "I can't think of even one rational explanation, can you? If I told anyone about any of it, I'd probably be committed. This is just one more bizarre moment in your life, Famous."

"Well, what are we going to do now?"

"The answers obvious, isn't it? Find out who took the book, get it back, return to the forest, get rid of the monster, and save the day. Right, Jeremiah?" Ellie was smiling like she was enjoying herself. Jeremiah rubbed his head and nodded.

Famous stared up at Ellie in shock. "You sure make it sound simple—just find the book, return to the forest, and get rid of the monster. That's it, huh? So easy. Ellie have you lost your mind?"

Edmond looked at her and said seriously, "Ellie, we have guests coming soon and this is all just too much. Maybe we should call Jonathan. He might be able to help."

Ellie walked in the bathroom, rinsed the washcloth with cold water, and brought it back to Jeremiah. "Listen, Edmond. Famous and Jeremiah need us. Jonathon has classes to teach. He can't just come running every time there's a curse or spell that needs broken or lifted." She shifted back to Famous, "Where's that letter from your grandmother?"

"It's in my room, why?"

"Maybe she included her contact information. It seems to me it's high time for you to learn about your heritage. I'll go with you. Edmond, everything is ready for the guests and I'll be back in time to prepare dinner."

"I don't know El, I'm not sure I am ready for that," Famous replied.

"Well you better get ready!" Jeremiah exclaimed as he stood up. "Listen, we all know this has been quite a change for you, but this is your destiny, Famous."

"I thought lifting the curse was my destiny. Let me guess, whenever there's some bad spell or horrible curse, that will be my new destiny? I'm not convinced this is my destiny. I think somewhere there is someone else who is brave and… and… Oh, never mind." Famous sounded like she was borderline hysterical. She sat on the edge of Jeremiah's bed and took a deep breath.

Jeremiah stood and placed a hand on her shoulder. "You are brave. Look at all you've done. This is what you are meant to do. Deep down you know it, too."

Ellie sat next to her. "Besides, you've got me, Edmond, and a wizard—of sorts." Ellie laughed and bumped shoulders with Famous. "What more could you possibly need?"

Famous smiled and rolled her eyes. "Fine, I'll get the letter."

Famous got up and stomped to her bedroom. She picked up her apron and retrieved the letter. It was hot to the touch. She turned around to see Ellie was standing there. "Ellie, feel this." She handed the envelope to her.

Ellie grabbed it, "Okay, now what?"

"What does it feel like?"

Ellie felt the envelope, "It feels like paper."

"Just paper, nothing else?"

Ellie shrugged and shook her head. "Just paper."

"Because when I touch it, I feel an extreme amount of heat. Like my fingers are burning hot. You don't feel that?"

Ellie flipped it over and rubbed her hands on each side. "Nope. Just room-temperature paper. That's it." She handed it back to Famous.

"I don't get it. It must mean something, right? It's so hot." Famous opened the envelope and pulled out a large, yellowed paper. It was not a standard 8x11 sheet of paper, it was much larger. "Here you read it." She handed it to Ellie.

Ellie carefully unfolded the vintage looking paper and flipped it over to look at each side. "It's blank." She held it out to show Famous.

Famous grabbed it and flipped it over as well. "Why would she send me a blank, oversized piece of paper? This doesn't make sense." Famous looked at the paper, she flipped it over, and held it up to the light.

"Do you see anything?" Ellie asked.

"I don't think so." Both of them squinted their eyes and looked closer. "I feel like it's trying to tell me something, but it's just an old piece of paper."

"What do you mean? Do you feel like it's saying something? Maybe you should try listening to it. You know, like hold it up to your ear."

"Really? That sounds so stupid!"

"Just try it! Nothing makes sense anymore."

Famous put the letter next to her ear. Nothing happened. She looked at Ellie and rolled her eyes. "See? Stupid."

"Famous, seriously? You're not even trying! You need to concentrate! Try again, and this time, have a little faith."

Famous held the paper to her ear, closed her eyes, and listened. She heard nothing, but the paper or her fingers felt hot. And heat radiated from the amulets in her pocket. She pulled the letter away.

"Anything?' Ellie anxiously asked.

"Hold on, I have to try something." She pulled the amulets from her pocket. One was glowing, "I wonder…" Famous held the amulet close to the page and words began to appear.

My Dearest Famous,

The amulets are everchanging. What once was purity is now wisdom. It is within you. Follow the map to find the answers. This will lead you to your birthright and the book of wisdom.

Grandmother Angelica

"Anything Famous?" Ellie was staring at the page.

"You don't see that?" She held it up to her, "Ellie, please tell me you can see the words."

"No, honestly I can't. It still looks blank to me. What does it say?"

"Well it's super cryptic about a map that will lead me to my birthright and the book of wisdom. I don't see a map though." She flipped the page over and placed the amulet on it. "Hmmm."

"What?"

"Nothing, that's what." She tried each amulet. "Well dang, let's think about this. The note says the amulets are everchanging, what do you think that means? Maybe I'm not concentrating hard enough." She flipped the page over again and the words were gone. "The words are gone." She looked at Ellie and then back down at the paper. "I guess I need to really concentrate on these amulets and figure this out." Famous held them tightly in her hand and closed her eyes trying to visualize a map in her mind.

"I see the words, Famous!" Ellie screamed with excitement.

"Shhh! I'm trying to concentrate here!"

As Famous continued concentrating, eyes closed, Ellie stared at the page. It seemed to come to life. Pictures of rivers, trees, and some kind of path. It looked old—similar to what you'd find in an antique or junk shop. The lettering was some type of calligraphy.

Several minutes passed as the page filled with images. Famous felt faint and opened her eyes. She sat on the edge of the bed staring at the map. "So, you can see this?" she asked Ellie.

Ellie nodded her head and nearly whispered in awe, "Yes, I can see it. I have never seen anything like that before. It was like it was being colored by invisible crayons or something. Slowly, each detail appeared. It was quite remarkable. I—"

Suddenly, details began to fade from the page. "What's happening?"

"I don't know!" Famous frantically held the paper up to the light. The map began to become clear again. "Can you see it now? Can you see the map, Ellie?"

"Yes, but I'm not sure I understand. It was there, then gone, and there it is again. It doesn't make sense, does it?"

"I totally don't understand either, but when I held it down like this—" she moved the paper down, "—it looked blank." Just as before the words and the map disappeared. "But when I hold it up like this—" she raised the page toward the light and the words and images began to reappear, "—voila! I don't know if the amulets have anything to do with it or not."

"Well, put the amulets down on the bed," Ellie urged her.

Famous put the amulets down on the bed and lifted the page. It was blank. "I guess that answers that! I just hope I don't have to start all over again." Famous picked up one amulet at a time, trying each one separately, until she came to the fourth one. The words gradually began to appear. "Okay, so I don't need all of them for this particular task. Good information. I feel like there's gonna be a learning curve to this witch business."

Ellie sat next to her on the bed. They were looking at the map when Famous had a thought. "Do you think it's just the amulet's powers? I mean, if I handed you the amulet and the map… You get where I'm going with this, right?"

Ellie looked at her and threw out her hands! "Let's give it a try!" She practically pulled the page from Famous's hands. Famous put the amulet in her other hand. Ellie held the map up and nothing happened.

"Are you concentrating?" Famous urged. "Maybe close your eyes and visualize it."

"Okay, but hush! I was quiet when you were concentrating." She gave Famous a sarcastic smile because she knew it wasn't true.

Ellie closed her eyes and gave it her best, but nothing appeared on the page. "We're just going to have to face it Famous, I am not a witch."

"Well, that's unfortunate." They began to laugh. Famous held out her hand. "Here, give it back so I can read it." She took the amulet back as well. "I just thought of something. I wonder if everything needs a counterpart. So, if they get separated it will do no good for bad spell-casters like Daniel."

"And does the amulet work like that for any witch? Could it be a family thing? Or did your grandmother cast a spell for only you?" Ellie raised her eyebrows and cocked her head as the questions tumbled from her mouth.

"All good questions to which I have exactly zero answers."

Slowly, Famous held the map up and read out loud the words her grandmother had written at the top. She then began to look at the map and was impressed by the detail and colors as they appeared before her eyes. In the bottom left corner, a compass appeared with a tiny picture in the center. A box in the bottom right corner showed to be a legend unlike any legend she had seen before. It had normal stuff like trees, rivers, and such, but there were also strange things like a skull with crossbones, what looked to be a bottle of potion, moons, stars, and other oddities for a map.

The very bottom in the smallest of writing had a small paragraph written in her grandmother's handwriting.

This is your map Famous and it is everchanging. Hold on to it as if your life depends on it! Because it does!

"What do you make of that Ellie?"

CHAPTER TEN

POSSESSION

Edmond came into the room with Jeremiah following close behind. "What is taking you girls so long?" Ellie and Famous snapped their heads back to see the men standing in the doorway. "Wow, that's a cool map. Let me see it." He grabbed it from Famous's hand to look at it and it began to fade. Famous and Ellie looked at each other and laughed.

"What happened to the map?" Edmond asked with wonder in his eyes. "Jeremiah, what do you make of that?" He held the paper out for Jeremiah to see. "It's blank, but just a second ago, it wasn't."

Jeremiah stepped back and wouldn't touch it. And Famous noticed as much. "Jeremiah, why don't you have a look at it," Famous suggested curiously.

Jeremiah glanced at it again without touching it. "Yes. I see that it is blank, but I didn't see it before. Edmond was in front of me."

"Well, perhaps you should take it and give it a closer look. Hold it up to the light." She motioned to Edmond. "Hand it to Jeremiah, Edmond."

Jeremiah chuckled nervously and stepped back slightly. "No, that's okay, I can see it fine from here." He stepped back a little more.

It was like a lightbulb went off in Ellie's head and she began to understand what Famous was up to. "Jeremiah, are you afraid to touch the map?" Ellie mused.

"Don't be ridiculous. Why would you ask such a thing?" Jeremiah rubbed his head. "I think I'll get some water," he said as he quickly left the room.

"That was curious, don't you think?" Famous pondered. She grabbed the map from Edmond and followed Jeremiah who had gone downstairs and into the kitchen. Ellie jumped up from the bed and quickly followed behind. Edmond seemed quite baffled by the situation but also followed close behind the women.

"All right Jeremiah. It's time to explain. What's up? I haven't time for all of this mystery and intrigue," Famous said as she was standing next to the large wooden table tapping her foot in expectation.

Jeremiah had a glass in his hand and was filling it from the kitchen faucet. "I'm not sure what you're talking about," he uttered with a shaky voice. Jeremiah shut off the water and took a drink slowly. He lowered the glass and looked at Famous. His eyes were twinkling, and his cheeks were rosy red. The two stared at each other for a moment without a word like it was an old Western showdown.

Ellie, Edmond, and Famous stood there, waiting for Jeremiah to say something. The silence was deafening. Ellie could take it no more. A long, "Sooooo?" was all she could manage.

"You may as well spill it. I'm not going anywhere!" Famous stared at Jeremiah. He turned to fill his glass again and seemed to be contemplating his next words. He lifted his glass to take another drink. "I'm serious,

Jeremiah. You can refill that glass ten times and I'll still be standing right here!"

"It's your map Famous!" he blurted out.

Famous set the map on the table and her hand brushed the bottom corner. She saw a flicker of color out of the corner of her eye. It drew her attention away from Jeremiah. "Did you guys see that?"

Ellie and Edmond looked at her, then the paper, and back to her again. They both shook their heads indicating they had not.

Famous stared down at the paper. She began to run her hand across the page. Nothing happened until she set her hand down on the left corner where the compass was displayed. Each detail slowly appeared as if it were being drawn at that very moment. She watched as the colors became more vibrant. She thought it looked slightly different than before, but she couldn't be sure.

Ellie was looking over her shoulder. "Is it my imagination or does it look different like it has more details or something? I can't really explain what I mean."

"I was just thinking the same," said Famous. They both stared at the map for several minutes. Famous noticed the legend had changed as well. "It's everchanging. That's what the note says."

Edmond looked confused. "Huh, I don't get it. What note?"

"The note here on the bottom." Famous looked down and the writing was gone. "I don't understand. There was a note from my grandmother. Ellie, look. I just noticed the one at the top is gone as well."

"Now, it's truly your map. I wouldn't dare touch it before," Jeremiah said with emphasis. Famous, Ellie, and Edmond looked at Jeremiah as if waiting for an explanation. "You see, it's a magical map. Once you put your hand completely on the compass, you took possession of it. Now, it will give only you directions. There are times it will be precisely clear and times it will not. These are the times when the outcome will be less important than the journey."

Famous stared at Jeremiah and back to the map. She suddenly became curious and lifted her hand from the map. It faded away. Jeremiah walked to her and placed his hand on her shoulder. "It is your map and no one else's. That will never change until you relinquish it to someone else that is gifted. This is a magnificent gift your grandmother has given you. I am sure your first path will lead you to her. That, my child, will give you the answers you seek."

"What about the monster in the forest and your missing book?" Famous asked.

"I think it's all tied together. I may now collect my creatures and travel back to my little cottage. My work here is done, and I shall wait for you to come." He smiled and he began to turn away.

"But I don't understand. I thought I was supposed to go with you."

"As did I! But this changes everything. It is much clearer to me now and will be to you soon as well. You must find the book and then come to me in the forest." He walked to the stairwell, turned, and said, "I shall get my things together. I'll be off in just a bit. Monster or no, I'll be glad to get back home." He disappeared up the stairs.

Only a few short minutes later he returned with his little animal carrying case. "Did you get everything already?" Edmond asked.

"I did!" he replied.

"Can I give you a ride into town?"

"Yes, that would be kind of you." Jeremiah hugged Ellie and Famous stood up from the table. Her eyes were filled with tears as she hugged him with all her might. "You'll be fine Famous, and I'm sure I will see you very soon."

"But I'm scared and nervous that I won't find your book or find my way back to you," she cried.

He looked at her face and wiped a tear from her cheek. "You have your map, so you won't be lost no matter where it takes you. That is what matters." Jeremiah turned and walked out of the dining area and into the hallway. He opened the front door. "Edmond, shall we?"

"Be right there. I need to grab my keys." Edmond gave Ellie a peck on the cheek, grabbed the keys from the hook on the wall, and followed Jeremiah out the door.

CHAPTER ELEVEN

A Big Pot Of Chili

Famous rolled up the map and turned to Ellie. "Well, I guess that's my cue to get my stuff together. I should be on my way soon as well."

"Maybe you should stay another night and study the map for tomorrow. That way we can get you some food and stuff for you to take on the road. You can do your laundry, pack, and get prepared. You have to have snacks in case there is nothing available."

Famous sensed Ellie's sadness. "There is no sense in putting off the inevitable. I wish I had told Edmond to wait. I hate to ask him to make a second trip into town." Famous walked toward the stairwell.

"Ahh, no worries he won't mind. It's not far at all. But like me, he'll surely be sad to see you go." Ellie watched Famous walking up the stairs and called to her. "Do you need some help packing?"

"No, thanks. Shouldn't your guest be arriving soon?" Famous ran her fingers along the small handrail as she climbed the stairs for possibly the last time, her thoughts running wild with anticipation. It was remarkably similar to the way she felt not so long ago when she left home.

She thought back to that day in her little, tiny house back in New York. It seemed so long ago. She remembered seeing a sign, or maybe it was in a book at the library, about the days being long, but the years being short… or something like that. She thought about it for a minute longer and continued up the stairs. Another thought crossed her mind about the library. She hadn't checked in for what seemed like months. They were probably very worried about her back home. She hadn't checked her email or even turned on her phone for days.

She hadn't thought about her world before her journey, or how it had changed. It had been days since she thought about how much she missed her mother. Days since she dwelled on the great sadness. She had barely read in her mother's journals or written in her own. Had it been long, or had it just felt like it?

She reached the top of the stairs and mindlessly turned and wandered into the room Jeremiah had stayed in. It looked as if he hadn't been there. The linens looked clean and pressed. The room smelled of lavender or maybe lilacs. The room looked pristine—ready to receive its next guest.

Famous wasn't even amazed by little things like this any longer. She knew he waved his hand or whatever and it was done. Famous thought that he must have been in a hurry to not have cleaned the room manually. She remembered him telling her one time that life would be no fun if you just snapped your fingers and everything was done in seconds.

She closed the door and walked to her own room. Luckily, she didn't have much to pack. Her mother's journal was on her nightstand and she thought about reading some of it, but then decided it could wait until she was on a bus, train, plane, or, for all she knew, a donkey. That was a funny thought—attempting to read a journal on a donkey. She visualized herself on a donkey fumbling with the pages and couldn't help but laugh at the thought.

"Ellie says you're leaving us today," said Edmond.

Famous jumped and sucked her breath in. "You nearly startled me to death, Edmond. Geez, I could have had a heart attack." She had her hand on her heart. "My heart is still thumping." She wasn't sure but thought he had sneaked up on her on purpose.

Edmond tried not to laugh without much success. "I'm sorry, I figured you heard me coming up," he chuckled. "I'm going to fix up some lunch before I take you into town. Are you hungry?"

She shrugged. "I guess I could eat. I only need a little while to get my stuff together and I'll be down." Edmond turned to walk away. "Thanks Edmond."

"No different fixing for three than two, right?" He smiled but there was sadness in his eyes as he turned and walked out the door. "Take your time," he yelled as he began walking down the stairs. "I need a little while to myself."

Famous made her way through the bathroom, collecting her toiletries. She did a quick sweep of the closet and drawers for her remaining things. She stripped the bedding and suddenly wished she could snap her fingers much like Jeremiah and have the room ready in a moment's time. She grabbed new linens from the linen closet, ran the vacuum, and gave the bathroom a once over. *There*, she thought, *all done*. She grabbed her belongings and wondered if she would ever see this room again as she closed the door behind her.

Ellie was placing bowls on the table when Famous entered the room. "Anything I can do to help?" Famous asked. She noticed a bowl of grated cheese and another of diced onions. She also saw salt and pepper, saltine crackers, and a tub of butter. "Please tell me we're having chili. I love chili."

"Yes, ma'am," Ellie answered, "and everything is just about done. I had taken it out of the freezer last night to thaw for today. When I make chili, I make enough for like ten meals. I use that great big kettle over the fireplace to cook it. I add in Italian sausage, hamburger, a bunch of veggies, a couple different types of beans, and my secret seasonings."

"Sounds scrumptious!" Famous's mouth watered at the very thought of homemade chili.

"It's great to have meals ready in advance for the occasional surprise guests or for when I just don't have the time or desire to cook." Ellie wiped her hands on her apron. She saw Famous's backpack and felt sad but put up a brave face.

Edmond came from the kitchen with a big pot of chili. He placed it on the hot pad and announced, "Let's eat!"

CHAPTER TWELVE

DOPPELGANGER

Famous closed the door on the truck and waved goodbye to Edmond. She watched as he pulled away thinking back to how sad it had been saying goodbye to Ellie. Her mother must have felt the same way, but at least she knew where she was going. Famous did not.

She sat on a bench at a bus stop and studied her map. Then decided that her phone would be more helpful about now. She reached into her backpack and turned it on. She was grateful it had a full charge. The map had showed a path northwest of Dublin so she wanted to find a bus that would go toward Dublin. She should have looked before she left, but it was too late to think about it now.

A quick search on her phone showed there was a bus to Dublin in a couple of hours. Two hours seemed kind of long to wait so she did another quick search for a rental car company.

The closest one was about a mile away. She decided a mile was too long a hike for her and waiting for the bus would be better.

As she sat there waiting, a car passed that reminded her of Daniel's car. Moments later, it passed by again. Her heart began to race as she was reminded of the night he had kidnapped her. "Be fearless, Famous!" she loudly exclaimed to herself, hoping she had only imagined what looked like Daniel's car.

"Did you say something?" a voice behind her jolted her spine. She turned to see a young woman standing behind the bench. She was close to Famous in age with very dark, auburn hair that flowed past her shoulders. She looked remarkably like Famous. They could easily pass for sisters, if not twins.

"I...I...I didn't see you there." Famous stuttered. She was staring at her. The resemblance to the face she saw in the mirror was unbelievable. Realizing she must be staring, she figured she needed to say something more. "I was just talking to myself. It wasn't important."

"Oh. Sounded like self-encouragement to me." The girl smiled, walked around the bench, and sat next to Famous. "I do that too—you know, talk myself up or into doing something that scares me." She turned and really looked at Famous for the first time. "Wow!" She looked a little closer. "You from around here?" Her thick Irish accent said that she definitely was.

"Umm, no. Well, kind of, I guess," Famous replied. "It's a long story. You?"

"Ireland? Yeah. Here? No. A few hours from here. I'm on my way back from vacation. So, what's your long story? "

"I really haven't the time, but the short version is my birthmother was from Ireland. My mom raised me in the U.S. I'm sorry. I'm Famous. And you are?"

"Famous? Is that really your name?"

"Yes, and I think you're the first person that didn't ask what I was famous for," Famous laughed. The car that had only driven by moments ago passed by again. Famous eyed the car and became increasingly nervous. "Listen, I really have to get moving."

The girl noticed Famous looked very uncomfortable. "Someone chasing you, Famous?" the girl asked as she turned around to look behind her.

"Probably just my imagination, umm..."

"Destiny!"

"Destiny. Who's Destiny?" Famous mumbled as she looked past the girl for the car but didn't see it. She wondered if it had turned off. Maybe she hadn't seen it at all.

"Me. I'm Destiny!"

Famous's head snapped back to look at the girl in the face. *Okay, so we look the same,* Famous thought to herself. *But seriously her having the same name as her birthmother? Coincidences like that seem unlikely.* "Your name is Destiny? Seriously?"

"Yeah, why?" Famous just stared at her trying to think of what to say. Should she tell her? It was hard to think. She stared past her again causing Destiny to look back. "Is everything okay? You keep looking behind me like your expecting something to happen."

"It's nothing. I really do need to get going. It was... um... interesting meeting you, Destiny," Famous said as she looked at the directions to the car rental place and stuffed her phone in her pocket. She stood up and looked at the doppelganger one more time. She really wanted to know more about Destiny, but she needed to get away. "I'm going to rent a car. Perhaps I could give you a lift somewhere if you wanted to walk with me. I should warn you; it's a mile away."

"Doubt you're going my way. I'm heading toward Dublin. But it's a couple hours until I catch the bus, so I could walk with you a little way I suppose." Famous smiled but didn't say anything. She nodded her head in the direction she was going, and they started to walk.

Several minutes went by before either of them said a word. "Maybe we're related!" Destiny blurted out.

"I couldn't tell ya, honestly. It *is* uncanny how much we look alike." Famous felt like she was walking really fast, but Destiny seemed to be keeping up okay. "Am I walking too fast?"

"Not if you're in a hurry, I guess." Destiny smiled sarcastically at Famous.

Famous stopped to let her catch up. Looking ahead, she noted the beautiful green hills in the distance beyond the little town. A church that must have been a hundred years old caught her eye. The thick ivy climbed the building and had nearly claimed one entire side of the building. It was times like this she'd think of her mother. *Famous don't forget to stop and smell the roses.*

"Whatcha lookin' at?" Destiny had stopped next to her.

"It's really pretty here. I sometimes need to remind myself to look around and appreciate it. That church, wow! It's so different here than the U.S. Have you ever been?"

"Me?" she laughed. "I've never left Ireland."

"Really? That's crazy! The public transportation in Europe is awesome. Flying is so cheap if you just carry a small backpack."

The walk went very quickly, each taking turns babbling along about this and that and comparing childhood stories. They laughed together and soon it seemed like catching up with an old friend. It was not long when the car rental place came into view.

"So, I could drop you in Dublin," Famous offered.

"Are you going to Dublin?" Destiny asked.

"That direction anyway. What do you say?"

"I say, why wouldn't I? You don't look like a serial killer. That is especially good for me considering you look like me."

"I think you look like me."

They both laughed. "We will just have to agree to disagree, my friend."

Famous held the door for Destiny and walked in behind her. There was a short, stocky guy sitting at the small desk behind the counter. He wore a polo-type shirt with the car rental company logo displayed on it. He jumped up and walked to meet them at the counter. "How may I help you today? Do you have a reservation?" he asked.

Famous looked at Destiny and back to him. She had never really had a need for a rental car before. "Do I need to have a reservation?"

"No. Just most people call ahead or reserve on the Internet. What size car are you looking for?"

"Uh, small, I guess."

He began to ask a myriad of questions: name, phone number, address, and to see her driver's license. As she answered, he tapped along on the keyboard, putting he information into the computer. "How long do you need it for?"

"I'm not really sure. What are my options?" Famous was thinking that she obviously hadn't thought this through.

"Well let's see what's available." He tapped on the keyboard. "Tomorrow, we might have a compact available. I had a mid-size, but it was just reserved online. Just a sec, let me look at one more thing. Bad news! I have nothing available until tomorrow. Would you like me to reserve that?"

Famous was slightly irritated. He could have told her that in the beginning so as not to waste her time. "No, thank you," she said curtly.

Famous turned and walked out the door. Destiny didn't say a word as she followed Famous, looking back and scowling at the man the whole way.

"He could have told you that from the get-go. So, Famous, you want to ride the bus with me instead?"

"May as well. I don't want to wait until tomorrow. How long do we have to get to back to the bus? I don't even have a ticket."

"We better get going so you have time to get one. You probably can get one on your phone easy enough when we get to the stop. There might be a stop closer. Let me google it." Destiny found a closer stop and they walked to it quickly.

When it finally arrived, they climbed the stairs and boarded the bus, choosing a seat where they could sit together. Famous wanted to watch out the window, so she slid in first. They sat quietly watching the people board the bus. The driver closed the door and the engine revved as he pressed down on the accelerator.

"And we're off!" Destiny exclaimed.

It would take about six hours to get to Dublin with all the stops. Famous wanted to ask about Destiny's family. She still hadn't mentioned the fact that she had the same name as her birthmother. Famous figured that knowing two people with the same name normally would be a coincidence. Given the fact that if Famous darkened her hair a bit, she and

Destiny would look identical, the chances of it being a coincidence were likely thin.

The first half of the trip was uneventful. They made idle small talk back and forth about the scenery. Destiny informed Famous that it looked no different than most of Ireland. "If you've seen one castle, you've seen them all," Destiny laughed. "Where in the world did your mum come up with the idea of naming you Famous?"

"I don't know. She always said I'd be famous one day. I wish she would have told me what for." They both laughed. "What about you? Why did your mom name you Destiny?"

"I was named after my aunt that died just before I was born. She was my mum's twin, but I don't know much about her. My mum didn't really talk about her when I was growing up."

Famous sat quietly as she prattled on until she could no longer be quiet. "My birthmother's name was Destiny!" she screamed.

"I know! Geez, it took you long enough!" Destiny replied and then laughed.

CHAPTER THIRTEEN

MUMS THE WORD

"What?" Famous asked, confused. "Mawmaw Angelica sent me. You know, in case you couldn't figure out your map. The only thing is, I wasn't supposed to let you see me or talk to you. I was given specific instructions. I mean, she said we looked alike, but I did *not* expect identical. I saw you reading your map and figured it couldn't hurt to just chat for a second."

Famous was digesting her words. "So, this *whole* time you knew who I was? Is that essentially what you're saying?"

"Yep. Don't get mad because I'm already going to hear it from Mawmaw when we get there. They were going to send another cousin if you didn't figure out your map in a 'timely manner.' I could give you a little help. See, it's all crazy the way it works with learning lessons, blah, blah, blah. Anyway, they figured after the

Daniel fiasco you may have trust issues with total strangers and might trust someone who looks like they could be related to you. If you had any problems, I was supposed to discreetly nudge you. If you caught me following you, well it would be easy to figure I am not a danger to you."

Famous was contemplating what to say when Destiny continued, "You have no idea how many people are waiting to meet you. Mawmaw said she nearly had a heart attack when she saw you."

"Okay, what was your plan today?"

"I hadn't really saw you until today. I was watching from far away when I saw you in the truck with that Edmond guy. After he dropped you off, I was kind of sneaking up to take a little look at you when I heard you talking to yourself. At first, I really did think you were talking to me. Once I saw your face, I was like 'whoa.'"

"Yeah, I can totally understand that. So, what now?" Famous couldn't help thinking how alone she was just a short time ago. She thought she had no family and here she was, face-to-face with her cousin. They sat back to come up with a plan. A sly smile grew on Famous's face. "You know, maybe I'll just tell them I caught you."

"As if!" Destiny yelled with a big grin on her face.

"Fine, we can just tell the truth," Famous smirked.

"So, your truth idea didn't totally suck, but it was only because you were struggling with your map."

"Nope, I'm not admitting to that. I had totally figured out my map."

"Really? You think you did? Well, think again. I saw you fumbling around with it, rolling it up like it was a blueprint or something." Destiny held up a small metal case that looked like it had business cards in it. "This is my map." She clicked it open and it appeared to have a single business card in it. Then slammed it closed with her fingers and shoved it back in her pocket.

"That is super cool, I suppose. But I did take possession of it, so it was only a matter of time."

"Possibly." Destiny leaned back in her seat.

Famous watched out the window for a long time. When she glanced back, Destiny had drifted off to sleep.

The ride continued, and the bus stopping to pick up or drop off other passengers periodically. The green hills were glistening from a combination of rain and sunshine. Every once in a while, Famous saw small stone cottages with smoke coming from the chimneys. Occasionally, a herd of sheep dotted the grass in the distance. The old-world churches with bell towers held her attention until she lost sight of them. Architecture from years gone by had always interested her.

"Hey," Destiny nudged Famous. "What are you thinking about?"

Famous shrugged, "It's a lot, this whole witch thing. I had the greatest mom ever. My life was simple, even boring. I guess I'm just trying to remember how I got here." She looked back out the window to watch as the clouds grew heavy and rain began to pour from the sky. "Do you know what happened with Daniel?"

"Yeah, mostly, anyway," Destiny answered.

"He wants the amulets and I swear I saw his car earlier," Famous was nearly whispering. "I think he took Jeremiah's book."

The bus came to its final stop. Passengers collected their belongings and stood in the line to disembark. Destiny and Famous sat and waited for the end of the line to reach their seat. "Don't worry, Famous. You're heading in the right direction. It's probably best if we split up when we get to Dublin. Follow your map, ok, because I can't interfere." They followed the last few passengers off the bus and Destiny hugged Famous goodbye. "It's been so amazing, but mums the word?"

Famous smiled. "Yeah, mums the word. See you soon?"

"Definitely!"

Famous glanced away for only a second and when she looked back Destiny had disappeared into the crowd.

CHAPTER FOURTEEN

I Have Your Destiny.

Famous pulled her hood on, slightly hiding her face, and started walking. She remembered the library was not far and would give her a safe, quiet place to study her map. She was anxious to get off the street in case Daniel had followed her bus and took the stairs up into the library two at a time. She darted in and sat at an empty table in a corner away from all other people.

Rolling her map out on the table, it looked like a blank yellowed paper. She placed her hand on the compass and watched as it appeared. Taking time to memorize the path that she needed to take, she noticed that the Lewis would take her right near where she needed to go.

A shadow passed behind her and Famous quickly pulled her hand from the map. She looked back, but there was no one there. She thought it best to keep moving. She started to roll up the map but decided to fold it instead. She really needed to learn Destiny's trick to make the map so small. She put her backpack on and figured she would grab a snack and find the train.

Walking out of the library, she felt a tug on her backpack. She pulled away thinking it had caught on the door. It didn't budge. She looked back and Daniel was holding the strap to her backpack.

"Get away from me!" she screeched and yanked her backpack away from him. She rushed back into the library and he followed her in.

"You have something that belongs to me," he said. "I have something you want. I'm willing to trade."

"I knew it was you that took the book!"

"I have your Destiny in my hands," He laughed. "Think about that for a minute. I'll be in touch." With that, Daniel walked out of the library.

Famous stood there for a few minutes before it dawned on her that the "Destiny" he referred to was likely her cousin. She tore out of the library and looked in every direction, but Daniel was nowhere to be found. At this point, she knew the police wouldn't do anything. She had no proof he had taken Destiny or committed any crime. She needed help and knew just where to turn. She just hoped her map would lead her where she wanted to go.

Famous asked a local for directions to the train station, and she was on her way. She thought maybe she was wrong about Daniel having Destiny, but she couldn't take that chance. There was no time to waste. She looked at the map to determine which train she needed. It wasn't a long wait, but was about a half hour ride.

When she got off the train, she looked around to be sure she wasn't being followed. Famous found herself walking for what felt like an eternity. It was nearly dark when she got to the field.

Hoping her memory was correct, she reached her hand in her pocket and held the amulets. Concentrating on the picture in her mind. She turned into the field where there was a large rock formation that she imagined once stood as a building of some kind.

She hurried until she came to a small creek with a stone bridge. She crossed to the other side, racing the darkness.

Famous soon came upon a gate that had "Warning" and "No Trespassing" signs. Slowly, she opened the gate, walked through, and continued walking up near the top of the grass-covered hill. The cobble stone cottage was surrounded by a large group of trees.

It was quite a hike up the hill, but she went as fast as she could. It felt familiar to her like she had been there before. The lights were shining from the windows and she powered on until she reached the door. She used the big heavy knocker on the door to knock. The large door creaked open.

"Hello?" Famous called out and peered in.

"Famous, is that you?" The little old woman she had come to find out was her birth grandmother walked in the room from a hallway. "Oh, you've found us. This is wonderful. Come in! Come in and have some supper. I'm sure you're starved."

"There's no time. Daniel has Destiny!"

CHAPTER FIFTEEN

RIDDLE ME THIS

"Famous, Destiny is fine. What are you talking about?"

"It's a long story, but I saw Daniel and he said he held my destiny and…"

The old woman reached her arm around Famous's shoulders and began to guide her in the house. "Come in and tell me all about it." She said in a soft, loving manner. "Destiny is here so he's just trying to trick you. There is nothing to worry about."

Famous was frantic, "You must listen. He said he had her. If he doesn't, then he probably followed me to find you or… I don't know. I know he has the book—the one Jeremiah brought with him when he visited me. I know what he's capable of." She sounded manic, breathlessly talking a thousand miles an hour.

Just then, Destiny walked in the room. "Hey cuz!" she smiled and waved. "How's it going? I told Mawmaw everything. I just couldn't, you know, pretend or lie. I've never been good with mums the word."

"Or following specific instructions," Angelica scolded her and gave her a look.

Famous was in shock. She couldn't believe that Destiny was there and fine. "I…I…don't understand."

"Everything will be fine, Famous," Angelica consoled her. "Let me get you some tea." She quickly got up and scooted out of the room, nudging Destiny toward Famous on the way out.

Famous looked up at Destiny in the dim light. It was like looking in a mirror. She still couldn't believe it. She glanced around the room, taking it all in. A wall that seemed to lead down a hall was covered in pictures. The room was lit with candles. A light from what she guessed was the kitchen was shining around the swinging door frame that the older woman had gone through.

"So, what's this Daniel business you were talking about?" Destiny sat in a chair facing her on the sofa. "I heard your voice and came out but didn't catch what you were saying before I walked in." She looked at Famous and waited for her reply.

Famous ignored her question, staring at the wall full of pictures. "Family pics?" She stood up and walked around the coffee table. Walking down the hall she could see the obvious resemblance in generations of photos. Destiny followed her and watched Famous touch the glass covering several. She stopped at one picture that looked to be the oldest on the wall. "It's Angelica, the princess," Famous said and turned toward Destiny.

"Well, yes and no… a descendant anyway. That is why you were chosen to break the curse. Did you know Mawmaw was named after her?"

"Really? Wait, why me? I mean, why not you? You grew up with…" She threw her hands up as if to say "all of this."

Angelica came out of the kitchen with a tray filled with three teacups, a teapot, cream, and a bowl of sugar cubes. "What are you two girls talking about?"

"The princess!" Famous quickly answered. Famous followed Angelica back to the couch and watched as she poured them tea. "I have so many questions."

Angelica wiped her hands on her apron and straightened to look at Famous. "You'll have answers soon, dear. For now, come sit and let's have some tea. Sugar?" She asked as she placed a cup in front of Famous and one in front of Destiny. "We need to talk about why you thought Daniel had Destiny."

Famous told them about the library and her encounter with Daniel. "What else could I have thought? Maybe he just wanted to follow me here."

"Oh, he wouldn't dare come here," Destiny said loudly. "This is the last place he would ever come."

Famous looked at her confused. "Why do you say that? I don't understand. Shouldn't we be doing something? Jeremiah's book, the monster in the forest, and Daniel? And again, I have to ask, why me? Destiny has been around this her whole life. I am not even part of this witchy world. So why me?"

"That is why, don't you see? One with a pure heart. Because of your mom."

"I didn't even know her."

"Your mom, not your birthmother. You've never used spells of any type—good or bad. And you were raised in a kind and loving environment surrounded by only love."

"I don't get it." Famous took a sip of her tea.

"You will," Angelica said. "In time, you will. But for now, we have more important things to deal with. You need to get that book back and get rid of the monster in the forest, right?"

"Again, why me?" Famous whined.

"It's your destiny, simple as that," her cousin said as if it would suddenly make sense to Famous. "Listen, it's complicated. It all has to do with the last time you were here and what Destiny wanted for you."

"I've never been here before today."

Angelica stood up and straightened her skirt. She bent down to pick up the teacups and said, "Actually, you have. You were too little to remember and there's no time to talk about it now. Tonight, you will need to get your rest because tomorrow will be a full day. Then, soon you'll need to follow your map and get the book. Once you have the book you will have the answers you seek."

"Does everything always have to be a riddle for me to figure out?"

"We can't interfere with your destiny because it will change your path," Destiny explained.

"Destiny, hush!" Angelica's voice was stern. She looked at Famous and softened her voice to say, "Famous once you recover the book, I promise it will have all the answers."

CHAPTER SIXTEEN

THE BOOK OF WISDOM

"Okay you can't change my path, but can you at least tell me about the book?" Famous inquired.

"It's the *Book of Wisdom*—" Destiny began.

"Destiny!" Angelica chided.

"Mawmaw, I'm just saying that I would not go chasing after a book to get rid of a monster in the forest without the facts. Most people wouldn't even believe in a monster in the forest and you're asking Famous to deal with it with little information?" Destiny questioned her grandmother and turned to Famous. "It's a lot to take in," she said.

"Destiny has a very good point, it *is* a lot," Famous agreed.

"Things are different now Mawmaw than before when she was following her mother's journals to find out where she came from. She knew and trusted her mother. I think she needs to know the whole story about the *Book of Wisdom*. Famous, we know Daniel stole the book."

"Well, I figured that."

"No, not from Jeremiah. He stole it from the library."

Famous looked confused. "If he stole it from the library, how did Jeremiah get it? Or is that a different book?"

"Okay, here's what happened. Mawmaw went to the curse-lifting ceremony to help you, but also to keep an eye on Daniel. That's why she disappeared when everything went dark—she was following Daniel. Meanwhile, I was at Daniel's stealing the book. I gave it to Jeremiah to give it to you."

"I thought the book was just to lift the curse?"

"It is, kind of, but it's actually a really big book with spells, monsters, witches, and you name it. For someone with the amulets and a bit of power, it is also how to break those spells or create those spells and curses. It's a history book, our history book. It's—"

"And that is why, the riddles for the location of where those amulets were hidden were written in the book," Angelica cut her off before Destiny could finish her thought.

Suddenly it was starting to come together for Famous. "What does all of this have to do with the monster in the forest, and why did you give Jeremiah the book?" Famous asked.

Angelica arranged the cups and teapot back on the tray and picked it up. "That is what you have to figure out," she declared. "But not today because today we're going to fix a nice dinner together. Tomorrow is another day."

CHAPTER SEVENTEEN

CLOSE TO NORMAL

Famous, Destiny, and their grandmother had decided to make pizza. Destiny had flour nearly all over her. Which made them all laugh and started a small flour fight. This is what Famous missed most about her mom. The times they were silly and just being in the moment together. While cooking, they talked about Famous's childhood.

Angelica watched the girls chatting with so much joy. It had been a long time since she had two girls playing in the kitchen. It brought back memories of her daughters playing. Famous and Destiny were the spitting image of her girls.

When the pizza was done, they sat at the tiny dinette table and talked about family. Destiny added another slice of pizza to Famous's plate and then her own. "Famous, you'll meet nearly everyone tomorrow."

"Really? Who is nearly everyone?" Famous asked.

Angelica finished a bite before answering, "I have summoned the community. Just like when you were a baby, many are coming from near and far to see you. Once again to help, but this time not to find you a mother. This time to bring you back to the family."

Famous was thinking as she ate. She had so many questions. She wondered how different her life may have been if she'd grown up with her birth family. She couldn't even imagine a different life. Hers had been so awesome. Her mom was her best friend. She was happy to have had the life she had had.

Famous sat listening to Destiny go on about their meeting earlier. Destiny was laughing, even as she admitted that it did kind of freak her out how much they looked alike.

Famous helped clear the table while Destiny started washing the dishes. She could tell how familiar she was with where everything belonged. She could tell she had been in this kitchen a million times. It made her wonder if she grew up close by. "Destiny?"

"Yeah?"

"Did you grow up here? Where do you live now?"

"Mostly I grew up here in this house. Mom's house is only a short walk. It's on the same property. You'll meet her tomorrow. She didn't know you'd be here tonight. I have a room here, too, though. I bet that it's cool living in New York. I am definitely going to go there someday. What do you do there?"

"I work at the library… or at least I did. That reminds me, I really need to get some emails off. I haven't checked in lately. What do you do here for work?"

Destiny dried a dish and put it in the cupboard. "Oh, a little of this and a little of that."

Famous got the feeling she was evading the question and decided to just let it go. Her mind wandered as she watched her finish putting the dishes away. She was thinking of her life back home—the library and her little house—and whether her life would ever be that close to normal again.

Destiny shared her room with Famous. There were twin beds that she imagined had belonged to their mothers. The room was filled with childhood mementos. Destiny's bed looked unmade and messy. The bed for Famous had a purple duvet and was made up neatly. She looked around the room and it was exactly what she imagined her room would have looked like if she had had a sister.

CHAPTER EIGHTEEN

A Bizarre Day

Famous awoke to the sound of voices. She glanced over and noticed Destiny was still sleeping. She picked up her phone to look at the time. It was nearly 9:00 AM. She quickly checked her email, answered a few emails from friends, and sent one off to the library.

"Hey!" Destiny's voice startled her.

"Hey, did you sleep good? I was so exhausted I slept like a rock!" Famous exclaimed.

"Me too, like a rock. Sounds like the others have started to arrive. It's probably going to be weird for you, huh?"

"Yeah, it's a little overwhelming. I have so many questions."

"I can't even begin to imagine what it's like for you." Destiny sat next to her on the bed and put her arm around Famous's shoulders. "Well today is really going to be a bizarre day. Just wait and see. Sometimes not knowing is better than knowing."

"What do you mean by that?" Famous looked surprised by Destiny's statement.

"Oh, you'll see. Trust me," Destiny chuckled.

The knock on the door was followed by Angelica's voice saying, "Girls, it's time to get up and come to breakfast. Destiny your mom is here."

"We'll be out in a minute!" Destiny yelled. "It's about to get weird. Are you ready?"

"Honestly, I doubt my life can get any weirder."

"You'd think that, wouldn't you? C'mon, let's do this." Destiny grabbed Famous's hand and pulled her off the bed. Famous followed her out of the room. She could hear several voices coming from the kitchen. "Just so you know ahead of time, there will be like twenty or thirty of them all talking to you at once. You think you have questions? Ha! They have been waiting to see you again for all of your life."

"They could have just looked at you," Famous joked about their resemblance.

"Ha ha," Destiny said sarcastically. They walked into the kitchen. "Hello, ladies. Here she is!" She held her arm out as if she were presenting Famous as royalty.

Famous smiled and suddenly felt a little awkward in a room full of aging lookalikes. They were all staring at her. "Hi," Famous said softly.

"Wow, it's uncanny. You can definitely tell she belongs in our family," one woman said to Destiny. Destiny introduced her as her mother, also pointing out she was Famous's aunt. The woman turned to Famous, "Angelica didn't tell us you're practically Destiny's twin. I'm Darla."

"It is nice to meet you, and yes, it is definitely startling how much we look alike," Famous replied, beaming as she looked at Destiny.

Darla laughed. "Well, you don't sound alike!" Noting the obvious difference in her accent from the others in the room.

Famous watched as the women reminisced with each other. Talking about the last time they had gotten together and what was new in their lives. Each took turns introducing themselves and telling her where they belonged on the family tree.

A familiar aroma of cinnamon and orange filled the air. Famous immediately thought of Jeremiah. She glanced around the room and realized that there was a distinct lack of men. It seemed odd that there were none. She waded through the women and into the living room wanting to look at the pictures on the wall again.

Destiny watched as she left the room. She excused herself from the conversation and followed Famous. Famous was standing in the hall. She had a framed photo in her hand that she had removed from the wall. Destiny could see where it had previously hung, noticing the color change of the paint on the wall.

The photo was of their grandmother and grandfather. Destiny estimated they had been in their twenties at the time. "Mawmaw and Pawpaw in the old days," she said as she stood next to Famous. "I was pretty young when he died, but from what I remember, he was the best."

"Destiny, where are all the men? I mean the kitchen is full of women." Famous noted as she put the picture back on its nail. She walked down the hallway looking at pictures of families recognizing the women in several and one man that looked familiar, but she obviously couldn't have any idea who he was or why he might look familiar. The pictures were so old and mostly in black and white that it was not possible she knew the man. "I mean I see men here in the photos, but none of them are here."

"Most of the men in our family wouldn't come to summoning. You see—"

Angelica had stepped in the hallway, watching the girls. She heard where the conversation was going and cut Destiny off. "Girls, we need to be setting up soon. Let us get some food in you first." She wrapped an arm around each of their backs and squeezed them close to her. "I've waited for this day for so long." Her voiced cracked as she seemed near tears.

They walked together back to the kitchen. The counters and table had been filled with pastries and breads of all types. Stacks of napkins were carefully placed in several locations between each of the platters. Famous breathed in the scent of the freshly baked goods.

She walked through the women listening to bits and pieces of their conversations. Some had accents so strong she couldn't completely understand what they were saying. Famous picked up a slice of bread that looked very much like Jeremiah's cinnamon orange bread. The taste was nearly the same, but not quite. It was the icing that tasted different. She was deep in thought about the flavors when Destiny came up next to her.

"Good?" Destiny asked.

"It is. It reminds me of bread that someone else I know makes," she answered.

Famous was about to ask Destiny about the men when Angelica began to speak loudly over the other voices in the room. "Ladies it's time for us to be with nature and ask the universe to give our Famous safety on her journey." Everyone began to walk out the door that led outside behind the house.

Angelica went up to Famous. "You'll need your map and the amulets." Famous nodded her head and walked away from the crowd.

Destiny began to follow behind her, but Angelica grabbed her arm. "Destiny, you must be careful what you tell Famous because you don't have all of the information. You could lead her in the wrong direction."

"Okay, Mawmaw," Destiny said with an eyeroll.

Famous reappeared with her map and the seven amulets. She opened her hand to show her grandmother. The amulets looked to be the size of a quarter. Each amulet had different pictures or symbols and resembled what Famous imagined would be found in an old pirate's chest.

Angelica closed Famous's hand and squeezed it tight. "Keep them safe, child. They strengthen your power more than you could ever believe." She nudged the girls toward the door and followed them out.

The others had gone to the top of the hill. A pentagram of stones had been laid there years before. The rocks had sunken into the earth, and mother nature had covered them with a velvet blanket of moss.

The crisp air was heavy and a thick fog hid the women from anyone at a distance. They stood in a circle surrounding the pentagram. Famous shivered as she climbed to the top to join the others.

Destiny was close on her heels. She reached out and took Famous by the hand to lead her into the center of the circle. She whispered, "Open your map, take off your shoes, and stand on your map with bare feet. I've been chosen so I'll be going with you today."

"Going with me? Where?"

"You'll see. Place your amulets around us and repeat the words they tell you. You must concentrate."

"Concentrate on what? I don't understand. Going with me? What do you—"

"Shhh! You'll be fine," Famous heard her grandmother whisper sharply.

Famous did as she was told and opened her map, removed her socks and shoes, and stepped onto the cool paper. She could feel the damp earth beneath the map and hoped it would not damage it. She took the amulets and placed them on the ground surrounding them, looking up each time for a nod of approval from her grandmother.

She stood waiting as the others began to chant. The words were not clear to Famous. She concentrated on the sound of the chant and felt compelled to speak. The words seemed to just fall from her mouth as if she had no control. "Give me guidance to a safe path. Use my gift of power to lead me to the *Book of Wisdom*." The amulets began to shine brighter and brighter as she repeated the words.

The chanting grew louder, and at times, she could only make out words like *safety* and *journey*. The light from the amulets had become blinding. She felt dizzy but continued to repeat the words over and over. The light intensified and was so blinding that she longed to close her eyes. Seconds later she was in complete darkness.

Really? she thought. *This again!*

CHAPTER NINETEEN

HURRY WE'RE RUNNING OUT OF TIME!

Famous opened her eyes. She was laying on the ground. She sat up and looked around. She could hear voices but couldn't make them out. It was no longer dark, but she was in the middle of a cloud. She couldn't see where the voices were coming from. She could barely see her hand in front of her face. Feeling too weak to stand she squinted her eyes to try to look around her, but it was useless.

She was feeling the ground around her when a hand on her shoulder made her jump. "Are you okay?" a familiar voice whispered to her. It was Destiny.

"What happened?" Famous whispered back.

"Well, we're kind of in your map." She could hear Destiny's words but couldn't see her at all.

"We're what?" Famous screeched.

"Shh! We are in your map. Take my hand," Destiny responded. It was almost like Destiny was there but also wasn't. It seemed like they were floating more than walking. The map appeared below them. Famous could see a dotted line. Destiny pointed at it and asked, "You see that line?"

"Yes. I don't understand how this is happening," Famous answered sounding nervous and scared. Her eyes followed the line. She could see the skull-and-crossbones symbol a short distance away.

The girls came to a fork in the path. "Which way? Do I follow one and you the other?" Famous wondered aloud.

"No," Destiny hissed. "Do not let go of my hand. This is your map. I could get trapped."

"Trapped? In the map? You would think that's information I should have known about ahead of time."

"Yeah, you'd think so, but rules are rules."

Other symbols for trees, waterways, and some things Famous couldn't recognize appeared as they drifted along the path. At the very edge of the map, extremely far way, a golden light shined brightly.

"Ah ha! There it is!" Destiny whispered as she altered their direction.

"What is that?" Famous asked as she stared at the golden haze.

She was beginning to see Destiny's face. The fog was lifting. "It's the *Book of Wisdom*. Hurry, see if you can read where it's located. We're running out of time."

Famous could see it was far away across an ocean, or was it an island? She squinted her eyes and strained to see. "I'm not sure. I think it's Greenland."

Voices began to get louder and clearer. The cloud was dissipating, and the map was disappearing. Destiny was holding her hand, and once again, they were standing on the hill surrounded by the ladies. Famous's knees were weak and threatened to give out on her.

Destiny nudged Famous and gestured for her to look down. Famous looked at the ground. Her map had shrunk down to business card size. She picked up her map. Then, snatched up each of the amulets.

The chanting had stopped, and they gathered around to hear about their experience. Angelica was the first to speak. "Did you find it?" she asked.

"We think so," Destiny answered. "It looks to be far—extremely far away. It's all the way at the edge of the map. Famous thought it said 'Greenland.'"

"I'm fairly sure. I'm good at geography, but it was so far away and hard to read."

Angelica stepped back with a look of dismay on her face. "How could it have been taken so far away?" She knew that journey would be hard for Famous, and she couldn't send her off on her own. The only one in the family fit and able to make such a journey would be Destiny. But Destiny was an undisciplined witch that didn't always follow the rules. Angelica shook her head, turned, and walked down the hill. Famous looked at Destiny who motioned for them to follow as the other women stood and whispered amongst themselves.

"Why does she look so upset?" Famous whispered to Destiny.

"Probably because it's so far away. That will be a hard journey for you," Destiny answered.

"Oh, great! I hadn't thought of that. How many times have you done that whole map thing?"

"First time. I was actually a little surprised it worked." She smirked at Famous.

CHAPTER TWENTY

THE TALK

The girls tromped down the hill following Angelica. Destiny grabbed Famous and pulled her back whispering, "I don't think that went as well as she hoped."

"It went exactly as it was supposed to. Only the outcome was unexpected," Angelica spoke sternly. She was a wise woman with many years of knowledge about the mystical world from the generations of their family that came from it. "We just have to figure out where we go from here."

"Greenland?" Famous questioned meekly.

"Exactly!" Destiny exclaimed excitedly. She leaned over and whispered to Famous again, "Don't worry. I'm going with you." She had whispered so quietly Famous barely heard her, but Angelica heard her loud and clear.

"Yes, Destiny, you are going with her, but only after we have a *long* talk."

Destiny squeezed Famous's hand, winked, and smiled. She looked absolutely giddy. "Greenland doesn't sound so bad Mawmaw. Of course, what do I know about travel?"

"You're not going on holiday," Darla called out from behind them. "Destiny this is serious!"

Famous glanced back to see Destiny's mother right behind them followed by all of the other women. "What happens now, Destiny?" Famous asked. She had figured she'd drop by, meet the family, and… that's where the thought had ended. "Find the book, go back to the forest, and get rid of the monster." Famous hadn't realized the words came out of her mouth as she was thinking them.

"New mantra, Famous?" Destiny laughed.

"Oh, I was just thinking out loud, I guess. It was something my friend Ellie said. She said it like it was so simple. You would have had to be there to appreciate the situation."

They followed Angelica into kitchen through the back door of the cottage. Several women followed in behind talking about random memories and how good it had been to see each other. Several offered small pieces of advice to Famous, but nothing too consequential.

After hours of stories and mindless chatter, Famous snuck out of the cottage and sat alone on a stone bench in the garden.

"I've been looking for you everywhere," said Darla.

"It's always the last place you look," replied Famous.

Darla laughed. "That's because you stop looking once you find what you're looking for." She sat next to Famous. "Too much for you?" She nodded in the direction of the cottage.

"I guess you could say that. In my real world—well, up until the last few weeks—I lived in a tiny cottage in a tiny town. I worked in a library, and if I wasn't reading stories about the world, I was making up a world of my own in the stories I wrote. Back then, I never could have imagined what I'm doing now."

"You are so much like me. Not Destiny. She was every bit like my sister. I don't know how you refer to her. She was your birthmother, but not your mom. You would have loved her.

Everyone did. If you spend enough time with your cousin, it will be like you knew her too."

"It's strange, you know. I am really struggling with the whole thing. I wish I could have known her, but my childhood was perfect. I know if I had been raised here, I would have been happy. I can see that. If only you could have met the woman who raised me, you would understand."

Darla smiled. "The fact that she was chosen was enough for me. It was hard not to keep you. I hope you know that. We were always watching in our way. It's hard to explain our ways to someone who is gifted, but never lived the life. You belong here now, but you needed to be raised far away from this world. You are a new beginning for us, and we are a new beginning for you. This is the way it was always meant to be."

"I'm grateful and sad at the same time." Famous had been struggling with this a lot over the past few days and was glad to have someone to talk to about it. "I have to be honest, I don't even know what to call Angelica… or you. I

avoid directly addressing Angelica. It is all so—
"

"Overwhelming?"

"Yeah, overwhelming. Since my mom died, I hadn't really thought about family or how I'd feel if I met my birth family. I haven't talked to anyone, so this is all totally weird for me. I had my mom, and then she was gone. Her journals brought me here."

"Well, Angelica met your mom before you went to the States and she cast a spell on those journals. But that is for another day. You call us whatever makes you comfortable. You can call me Aunt Darla or just Darla. We have known about you for your whole life, but we are new to you." Darla put her arm around Famous and hugged her.

"Okay, 'Just Darla,'" Famous giggled, "what's next?"

"Part of your destiny is to get the book. It's actually more important to you than you know. But it will be a hard journey and the only thing we can do is send someone with you to help. The only one fit enough and able to go is Destiny. She is so much like your mom—a breath of fresh air, carefree, and just plain fun to be around." Darla sighed. "We are concerned. She is undisciplined. She breaks the rules. We worry that may be more of a hindrance than a help. We are not sure if you would be better off on your own. It's your decision, but either way, you need the book."

Destiny appeared out of nowhere. "There you two are," she said. "Hey Mom. Mawmaw has been looking for you, Famous. She wants to talk to you about the *Book of Wisdom*."

Famous got up from the bench and started walking to the cottage. She turned back and said, "Thanks for the talk, Aunt Darla."

Darla smiled and nodded. "Of course, Famous. Anytime."

CHAPTER TWENTY-ONE

EVERCHANGING

Destiny followed Famous into the cottage. "Mawmaw, I found her," she called out when they entered the door.

Angelica came from the kitchen. "There are some things I must tell you, Famous, before you start off in the morning." She sat on the couch and patted the spot next to her. "Come, child. Sit with me."

Famous did as she was told. Destiny started to walk to the kitchen, but her grandmother stopped her. "You need to hear this as well, Destiny!" she yelled. Destiny sat next to Famous and Angelica began her story.

"Many years ago, the *Book of Wisdom* was created by a great wizard. His name is unimportant at this time. This wizard had many generations of children and the book has passed through each one. It has been the cause of happiness and destruction in many lives. The same wizard created the maps that you both have. We are unsure how many maps exist. The map is only useful to the one who has possession of it. Once they relinquish the map by spell or death, it waits for a gifted person to take possession. The book and these maps are everchanging because of an extremely rare spell that allows them to change with the time and situation—"

"So they're always different?" Famous interrupted.

"Several things in the book are written in stone, meaning they will never change. Those are as important, if not more important, than anything else. The monster in the forest must be released. It is written in the book, but only you, Famous, have the power to release it."

"Why me?"

"That, my child, I cannot tell you."

"Is it because you don't know or because you're not supposed to?" Destiny asked, her voice insinuating it was one of those rules she felt were unnecessary.

Angelica continued as if Destiny had not spoken, "Given the right ceremony, the maps will always lead to the book. We believe that is how Daniel found the book. He may have gotten his hands on a map. But we are unsure."

"Does that mean I will always be in danger if I have the book?" Famous asked. "Am I keeping the book after I release the monster? Do I really want to release a monster into the world?"

"Famous, it's really difficult to answer all of your questions as there are more than one possible answer for each question."

"I don't understand." Famous was confused by her grandmother's words.

"It is everchanging—a question may have one answer today and yet another tomorrow."

"That doesn't make sense!" Destiny interjected.

"Let's start with this question because I feel like the answer will always be the same," Famous stated. "If I get the book, does that mean that while I have it, anyone with a map that wants the book will come after me?"

"Possibly yes, possibly no. There are other considerations," Angelica answered.

Famous waited thinking she would elaborate, but she did not. "This is all very complicated!" Famous felt exasperated.

"When things change, so will the outcome. Although the question is the same, the answer may not be, given the different situation." Angelica got up from the couch indicating they were done with the conversation. "I better get some dinner on. You will have a long day tomorrow. I'll leave you two to talk." She started to walk into the kitchen but turned for one last thought. "I will give you an example. It was written that you would return to the forest and release the monster and that will not change, but at that time, Jeremiah had the book. That is why we took the book from Daniel and sent it to him. It has since been stolen from him. Now, the book has changed. It has been added that you must find the book before you return to the forest to release the monster." Angelica nodded her head, turned, and went to the kitchen.

"Yeah, that cleared it all up." Destiny's sarcasm was obvious as she looked at Famous. "Did you get that at all?"

CHAPTER TWENTY-TWO

DECISIONS OVER DINNER

"You know when I worked at the library, I read thousands of books," Famous remarked. "And I am not exaggerating either. I was always excited when we got new books. I can honestly say this is the first time I am not excited about a book."

Destiny laughed, "I can understand that. Hard to believe this is my normal, isn't it?"

"Definitely. You know, I'm leaving tomorrow. I guess I am just going to head Northwest. See if I can catch a ship or plane to Greenland."

Destiny was about to speak when their grandmother called them for dinner.

"Oh good, I'm famished!" Famous exclaimed as she stood up and headed to the kitchen.

Destiny followed Famous. Darla must have come in the back door because she was helping to put dinner on the table. Plates had been set for the four of them.

"I'm sorry I missed saying goodbye to everyone," Famous said as she had just thought of the kitchen being so full of women earlier that day.

"Oh, don't worry. It's fine. I'm sure you will certainly see them again one day," Angelica said matter-of-factly. "Come sit at the table girls."

Famous watched as Darla dished meatloaf with mashed potatoes on each of their plates. Then, she filled their smaller plates with salad.

Famous shoved a bit of meatloaf in her mouth and made a "mmm" noise. "This is really good," she marveled. "It's different from normal meatloaf but tastes like my mom's. Tomato sauce instead of eggs?"

"Yes, I've never cared for eggs in my meat," replied Darla. "But you need something to help bind it, right?" Darla seemed pleased Famous was enjoying her cooking. "I've always made it this way."

They ate in silence for several minutes before Angelica spoke. "Famous have you made any decisions on your travel plans?" she asked.

"So far, not really. Nothing other than I am leaving in the morning. I need to be done with all of this monster business."

"And then what?" Destiny asked mindlessly. Famous, Angelica, and Darla all stared at her. "What? I was wondering if she knew what she will do after." Destiny shrugged.

"I haven't had time really to give it a thought. I guess we will have to see when it's done." Famous shoveled another bite in her mouth.

"Speaking of that, I plan to go with you in the morning. It makes sense for you to have someone with some understanding of the map and our ways. I think so anyway." Destiny was excited about taking a trip and had thought about it all day.

Darla offered more to everyone before beginning to clear the table. "Famous will have to have time to think what's best for her," Darla said.

"There is no time. She's leaving in the morning. I'll need to pack," Destiny pointed out. "Famous, I swear I will help you. I do take this seriously, no matter what they think." She put her hand up indicating her mom and their grandmother didn't have faith in her.

Angelica began helping Darla clear the table as Famous finished her salad. Destiny waited for someone to say something, but no one did. "It's not like she can just jump on a plane to Greenland, follow the map to the book, find a way to get it and head back to the forest!" Destiny exclaimed.

Famous looked up from her salad. "Why not?" she asked. "It sounds like a good plan."

"It's not that simple, that's why!" Destiny spouted as she picked up her plate and walked to the sink. "You don't even know who has the book and who may be following you along the way. You will need to be careful. The monster in the forest is like Pandoras Box. It—"

"Destiny that's enough!" Angelica roared. "You do not have enough information to try to explain. Famous, what she is trying to say is, it's best to fly under the radar. Take transportation that isn't on the Internet for any hacker to find. Follow your map, watch for the dangers, and watch your back."

"When you traveled before, every time you bought a ticket, Daniel surely knew," Destiny said. "He used that information to get you to come to him and help him find the amulets, by making you think he was helping you. You have to think of it like someone is out to get you. I am perfect at being devious and that is why I should go."

"She does have a point!" Darla pointed out, sitting next to Famous. "But it is up to you to decide what is best for you, Famous."

Famous thought about it for a while as she helped Destiny with the dishes. She wanted to have someone with her, but worried about Destiny's mischievous behavior. She handed Destiny another plate to dry.

"I do really want you to come," Famous started, "it's just that I am worried. If you promise to not get me thrown in jail or killed, I think it will be good to have you along."

Destiny grabbed Famous and hugged her excitedly. "Deal! I promise not to get you thrown in jail or killed!"

"Then, we leave in the morning."

CHAPTER TWENTY-THREE

WHAT WAS THAT?

The night went quickly. After dinner, they sat and made plans for their departure. Angelica and Destiny helped to make arrangements to get them a ride to the west coast of Ireland without detection. It would be a challenge. They knew that given the right knowledge anyone with a map and some power may be able to find the book. It would be safer if they didn't have someone right on their heels.

"How many people have a map?" Famous asked.

"We don't know," Angelica answered. "I'm not sure anyone knows how many were cast before the spell was removed. There may be only the two you girls have. There could be hundreds. I would think the only way to know is to consult the *Book of Wisdom*, and even that's not certain."

Destiny took Famous with her to her house so she could pack a backpack. As they walked the path, Famous asked if she would be meeting Destiny's dad. Destiny had a flashlight and shined it back at Famous. Famous closed her eyes and held her hand out.

"Sorry, I didn't mean to shine it right in your eyes," apologized Destiny. "I was surprised by the question. I thought my mom had told you he is away."

"No, she didn't mention it. Like on business?"

"Like that, but maybe he will be here when I return." It was strange the way she said it, but either Famous didn't notice or she didn't acknowledge as much.

It hadn't been a long walk when they came to a tiny cottage. They followed the dirt path to the door. Destiny opened the door and welcomed Famous inside. It was much smaller than Angelica's cottage. It was tasteful, uncluttered, and more modern than Angelica's as well. The living room was decorated in teal and gray. There was a gray couch with teal throw pillows and a gray end table between two teal accent chairs.

"I only need a minute to pack," Destiny said as she darted out of the room. "Make yourself at home."

Famous walked past the couch and into the adjoining kitchen. There was a small island in the center of the kitchen. The counters were marbled slate gray and white. The kitchen was spotless and looked rarely used. There was nothing on the counters—no coffee maker or kettle… not even a salt and pepper shaker.

"Famous, do you have a warm coat with you?" Destiny called from the other room. "It's going to be cold—probably freezing."

Famous followed the voice and walked into Destiny's room. The room was decorated the same as the room she had slept in the night before. Three of the walls were covered in hand-painted murals that looked like pages in a story book. The pictures were mystical. There was a woman dressed like a wizard with a wand following a path on one wall. On another wall, the same woman was sitting with a crystal ball at a table with an older version stirring a cauldron hanging above a fire behind her.

"Wow, this is cool. Who painted it?" Famous asked.

"Me," Destiny replied. "It's not finished. I still have to add more detail and there's one wall I haven't started yet. After I'm done, I will add the story."

"It's stunning. You're so talented and skilled. That woman even looks like you. I would have thought it would be difficult to paint yourself. I bet it will be a great story."

"We'll see. It's just a hobby, that's all." Destiny was dismissive. "Do you need a warmer coat?"

"I think I'm okay." Famous couldn't stop staring at the walls. They were mesmerizing. "Destiny this is really good. I mean, unbelievably good. Don't sell yourself short."

"Thanks. Maybe I'll finish it someday. We need to get going."

Suddenly, Destiny felt a chill in the air and yanked Famous's arm, leading her through her room toward the door. "We need to go!" Destiny yelled as the cold air hit Famous who shivered. Destiny was practically dragging her now.

"What wrong?" Famous asked when the amulets began to burn in her pocket.

Just then, Destiny ran and picked something up that she had set down with her house key. She held it tightly and raised her hand. It was a medallion shaped like a pentagram on a long chain. "Show yourself!" she shouted. Famous looked around the room. "I know you're here. Show yourself."

With that, the door flew open. Famous felt herself being knocked to the floor and screamed.

Destiny ran to her. "Are you okay?"

Famous looked a little dazed. "Yeah, I just got the wind knocked out of me. What was that?"

"I'm not sure, but we need to get out of here. I should never have taken my necklace off. I'll explain later. Let's get back."

"Is it safe?"

"Do you feel safe here?"

"Good point!"

"Give me your hand, Famous, so we don't get separated."

Famous grabbed Destiny's hand and they ran out slamming the door behind them. It had gotten dark outside. Famous couldn't see. She held onto Destiny's hand trusting Destiny would get her back to their grandmother's safely. They ran—their hearts pounding and breathing hard.

"Destiny, I have to stop! I can't—" She stopped and bent over. She had her hands on her knees and the amulets began to burn again.

"Famous, c'mon! Now!" Destiny grabbed her arm. Famous wasn't sure whether it was a sudden burst of energy or straight out fear, but she found the strength and kept running.

When they reached Angelica's, they were ready to drop. They charged in the back door and slammed it behind them. They startled Angelica so much that she charged into the kitchen.

"What's happened?" Angelica asked. Both girls were breathing too hard to answer. "Come, sit down." Angelica walked to the table and pulled out the chairs. The girls sat down while Angelica got them each a glass of water.

Once she caught her breath, Destiny told what had happened.

"I thought you said Daniel wouldn't dare come here," said Famous, continuing to breath loudly with the words.

"He won't!" Destiny exclaimed.

"Then, what was that?"

Destiny shook her head and said, "Good question. Mawmaw, he wouldn't go to my house, would he? I mean, I know he won't come *here*. I always assumed that meant the whole property."

Angelica got up from the table. "First things first. Destiny, call your mom's cell. She went to the shop in town. Make sure she doesn't go home."

Destiny did as she was told. As she hung up with her mom, Angelica left the room.

"Where did Mawmaw go?" Destiny asked. Famous shrugged. "Let's go check."

They wandered through the living area and down the hall. The lights were off in every room.

"Did you notice which way she went out of the kitchen?" Destiny asked.

"I wasn't paying attention. I was looking at you," Famous replied.

"Hello?" a voice called from the kitchen. "Where is everybody?"

"Who's that?" Famous whispered.

"My mom silly. Are you freaked out or what?" Destiny laughed.

"Do you have any idea what kind of a week I am having? I guess you probably do, but still."

Darla was in the living area waiting for them. "Where's your grandmother?" she asked.

"We don't know. We were just looking for her," Destiny replied.

Angelica walked into the room. "Oh good," she started, "you're here and safe. Did they tell you what happened?"

"Destiny told me on the phone," Darla answered. "Good thing she caught me. I was nearly home."

Angelica held a book up and set it on the table. Darla looked at it and frowned. Famous also looked at the book.

"The Mystery of Witches and Magic Spells," Famous read aloud. She stared at it for a moment remembering something. "I've seen that book before. At least I think I have. No, I know I have. One thing I remember is books! I was at Ellie's in the bean bag room. I remember running my hand down the books and it felt like it called to me. I sat down to read it, but I fell asleep. I don't remember seeing it again after."

"Hmm, that's interesting," Angelica said. "Well, it doesn't matter tonight. You girls need to get showered and rest up before you go in the morning."

Destiny grabbed her backpack from the floor and motioned for Famous to follow her. Famous started to protest, but Destiny shook her head indicating for to follow her. "It will do no good, Famous," she said. "C'mon!" Famous followed reluctantly.

CHAPTER TWENTY-FOUR

A SAFE PLACE TO HIDE

Angelica waited until she heard the bedroom door close before speaking to Darla. "Could have been a helper showing her this book," Angelica said.

"Possibly a helper," Darla agreed. "It's too bad she didn't read it. Are you going to send it with her? The only problem with that book is a lot of it is fiction. Only bits and pieces might be at all helpful and we don't even know why she felt compelled to read it. What if it wasn't a helper, but the opposite?"

"As far as we know a lot of it is fiction. We don't know how much of it is true. I'm going to have to sleep on it. On another note, I think you should stay here tonight because of what happened to the girls at your house. It'll be easier for you to say good-bye to them in the morning if you're here. I'm going to go do a little reading. It's been awhile since I've read this."

A while later, Destiny and Famous came out to tell Angelica and Darla goodnight. Darla had since gone to bed. Once the girls were tucked into bed, Angelica sat reading the book until late in the night.

The house was eerily quiet when Angelica thought she heard a noise coming from outside. She looked out the window, but she didn't see anything.

Angelica walked back to the bedrooms. The light was out in Darla's room, but the light was still on in Destiny and Famous's room. She listened at the door and could hear the girls talking but couldn't make out what they were saying. She reached for the doorknob to go inside and talk to them but thought better of it. Instead, she walked back to the living area to shut off the lights. She'd take her reading bed.

As she turned off the last lamp, she could hear it had begun to rain outside. Thunder and lightning storms were rare where she lived. She couldn't remember the last time it had stormed. A thumping noise from outside startled her.

Angelica looked out the window. The wind was blowing hard and the trees cast swaying shadows in all directions. She calmed herself thinking it must have been the wind. Then, sudden knocking on the door caused her heart to skip a beat. She looked out the window from the hall and could not see anyone on the doorstep. Being a woman of wisdom, she knew better than to open the door. It can be considered an invitation to unwanted guests. The noises continued louder and louder.

Frightened, Angelica raced to Darla's room to wake her. Darla awoke and saw the terror in her mother's eyes.

"Don't turn on the lights," Angelica rasped. "We need to get the girls out of here!"

Darla didn't even question her. She quietly got out of bed and followed her mother out of the room. Thunder roared and the dark house was illuminated by a massive crack of lightning. It was so loud they were sure a tree had been struck nearby.

"What's going on?" Darla breathed and looked to her mother for answers.

There was more banging on the door and the windows began to rattle. Both women dropped to the floor out of sight of the windows. They crawled toward the girls' bedroom.

"I don't understand this has always been a safe place," remarked Darla.

"We'll talk when we get the girls downstairs," Angelica answered.

Slowly, they opened the door to the girls' room. The light from the bathroom was shining and Famous's bed was empty. Another loud bang came from directly outside the bedroom window. Famous came running out of the bathroom.

"Turn off the light, Famous!" Angelica hissed.

Famous saw them crouching on the floor and she felt uneasy. She turned, flipped the light out, and hit the floor. Destiny had awoken and was slinking out of her bed. "What's going on?" she asked.

"Shh! Follow me. Girls grab your backpacks," Angelica answered.

The four of them crawled out of the room one by one, Famous and Destiny dragging their backpacks behind them. They continued to crawl until they were inside the hallway bathroom. They stood as Angelica shut the door.

Angelica opened the towel closet. She pushed on something and then pulled the towel shelves open to reveal a staircase. She lit a lantern that was hanging inside.

"Here, take this," she ordered handing Darla the lantern. "Go down the stairs. You girls follow."

As Darla and the girls began their descent, Angelica didn't follow. Instead, she pulled the shelves back into place and bolted the door. Then, she pulled a wooden plank down to further barricade the hidden door, securing them from the inside.

Once they reached the bottom of the stairs, they stood there waiting for Angelica to make it all the way down. Famous noticed it had grown quiet. The hidden room was enchanted to block all noise from travelling in or out. The storm was raging on outside, but they couldn't hear a thing.

Angelica flipped on a light and it illuminated a large room. Famous, Destiny, and Darla surveyed the space. One wall was completely filled with books. *Those are probably spell books,* Famous thought. Another wall had bottles of all sizes with strange lettering. Famous imagined they must be potions of one kind or another. There was also a cauldron.

Finally, Angelica spoke, "We seem to have some uninvited guests outside. Right now, this was the only way to make sure you all are safe. We will ride out the storm down here. Just before dawn we will take the tunnel and sneak you out."

"Sneak us out?" Famous and Destiny asked at the same time with puzzled looks on their faces.

"The tunnel?" Darla asked looking even more stunned.

"You're not safe here. You won't be safe until you have that book and you're with Jeremiah."

Destiny looked at her mom and back to her grandmother. "What about you and mom?" she asked.

Darla put her arm around her. "Don't worry about us. We will be safe when you two are gone," she promised.

Darla's promise didn't make the girls feel any better. Darla turned to Angelica and asked, "Has this room always been here?" Famous and Destiny were surprised that Darla didn't know about it.

A thought suddenly occurred to Famous. "This is where you disappeared to earlier, when Destiny and I were looking for you," she thought aloud.

"Yes, it is. To answer your question, Darla, your father built this room. Back then, if you were caught with—" Angelica waved her hand around the room as she spoke, "—this type of stuff, it could have had serious repercussions. It's kind of a long story, but it doubled as a root cellar during hard times. The tunnel was put there for us to escape during the wars if we needed to. It's been years since I walked the tunnel. I hope it's held up."

Famous walked around the room looking at the books and the weird odds and ends on other shelves and tables. One wall had shelves filled with food. She noticed photo books and boxes of loose photographs. She began to leaf through them. Another box caught her eye. It had *Famous* written on it. She started to open it when Angelica stopped her.

"That's for another time," Angelica warned and picked up the box, moving it to a top shelf above the books.

"What's in it?" Famous questioned.

"Just some old mementos that are to be passed down to you. There's one for Destiny around here somewhere, too."

Famous went back to the box of photo books. She pulled one out. The pictures were the oldest pictures she had ever seen. Destiny had gotten curious and was looking over her shoulder. The next book was of Darla and Destiny (her birthmother) as children. They looked at each page and whispered back and forth, giggling every so often.

Angelica and Darla sat in some old chairs talking about the next plan and whispering so the girls couldn't hear them. Angelica found some old bed rolls and laid them out. "We should try to get some rest," she announced to the group.

CHAPTER TWENTY-FIVE

THE TUNNEL

Famous was running and screaming for Destiny. She was frantic. It was dark in the forest. She kept running. Was something chasing her? She looked back and called out, "Destiny, where are you?" The words rang out through the dark room.

Destiny shook her awake, saying "I'm here, Famous. It's only a dream."

Famous, sweaty and breathing heavy, sat straight up and looked all around her trying to figure out where she was.

Angelica and Darla sat next to Famous. Tears began streaming down Famous's cheeks. "A dream. It seemed so real," she said. "It was awful. I couldn't find you. I was so scared that you were gone forever."

"It was just a bad dream. That's all it was. You're safe," Angelica assured her as she stood up. "I'm fairly sure I have an old kettle and some hot chocolate down here. Let me take a look." She found a box of hot chocolate packs and the kettle and started digging around for cups. "I keep so much junk, you would think I have some coffee mugs around here somewhere."

"It's okay. I'm okay," Famous said. "It was only a nightmare. I had one similar at Ellie's. I was just thinking about that. It made me think of something. It seems like anytime I'm in danger the amulets seem to warn me. I'm not sure how it works, but when you came in the room tonight, the amulets weren't hot or lit up."

"Maybe it's because as long as you're in this house, you're safe," Destiny said. "I'm no expert though. We don't know how the amulets work. We all have something that gives us more power. You will, too, when you find it—or it finds you. We think the amulets are kind of universal."

"They are mentioned several times in the *Book of Wisdom*," Angelica said. "But they were with Daniel's family for hundreds of years until your birthmother took them." Angelica looked at her watch. "I think it's time to check out that tunnel."

Darla, Destiny, and Famous got up to follow Angelica.

"When I find the book, what will I do with the amulets?" Famous asked. "And how will I find my, for lack of a better word, lucky charm? I'm not really sure what else to call it."

"We all have different stories on how we got our charms, but that is for another day. Let's go." Angelica started toward one of the bookshelves.

"Where does it lead?" Darla asked. "The tunnel. Where does it come out?" Angelica didn't answer her. She put her hand behind one of the books on the bottom shelf and pulled a lever. Nothing happened. Famous, Destiny, and Darla bent down to watch. She tugged on the edge of the bookcase several times, but it didn't budge. She bent down and pulled the lever again harder. Then, she grabbed the edge of the bookcase and tugged at it. Darla went over and pulled, too, but still nothing. Famous and Destiny joined in and it wobbled a little.

"Maybe the lever isn't working," Angelica stated. "It's been years since it's been used. It could be rusted or something."

Angelica moved the books then pushed and pulled the lever several more times. Finally, she heard a *click*. She stood up and a door swung open.

"It shouldn't have been that hard," Angelica remarked. "To be honest, I never thought I was going to use this tunnel again."

Famous looked at Destiny and whispered, "Again?" Destiny shrugged. They looked down the tunnel. It was pitch black.

"Where does it go?" Famous asked.

Angelica was reluctant to answer, but she relented. "The pumphouse in the pasture," she said.

Darla looked at Angelica. "All the way down there?" she shrieked. "Are you crazy? The tunnel must be destroyed. There's no way there hasn't been a cave-in in all these years. I don't even want to mention the other issue."

"What other issue?" Famous demanded. She stood waiting for an answer, but none came. "What other issue?" she repeated.

It was Destiny who spoke up first. "Wow, where to begin? The tunnel comes out on someone else's property. Mawmaw sold that part of the property long ago and there's bad blood with the new owners. That's the short version of the story."

"Wel, it sounds like I need to hear the long version."

Angelica looked at her watch again. "Another time. We need to get going!" She walked up the staircase and removed the plank from the door then unbolted it. Darla started up the stairs.

"I thought we were going out through the tunnel. Did you change your mind?" Darla asked.

"No, but I plan on coming home above-ground. I don't want to have to come back through the tunnel to unlock this door."

Angelica rejoined them by the tunnel, then picked up the lantern and lit it. They all started down the tunnel, closing the door behind them. Famous tried to ask questions about the tunnel and the "bad blood," but her questions went unanswered so she gave up.

The group silently walked through the dark, damp tunnel. Tree roots had broken through in several areas. Angelica whispered warnings, pointing out tripping hazards.

They sloshed through water and mud. In one area, part of the tunnel had caved in, but with a little digging they were able to clear it enough to crawl through. They continued walking and walked for what felt like ages. Angelica shined the lantern on her watch to look at the time. She picked up the pace a little.

After nearly an hour of tripping over roots, crawling through muck, and digging dirt, they had come to the end of the line. Angelica felt around the bottom for the lever. Roots had broken through and grown over it. Darla began pulling them off and away from the lever, but one was extraordinarily strong and had grown into another crack. Famous dug in her backpack and pulled out a pocketknife. She began to saw away at the root until Darla was able to break it.

Darla pulled the lever and the door above them clicked. They took turns climbing up and out of the tunnel into the pumphouse.

The pumphouse was dark and only dimly lit by the dawn of the sun peaking in around the exterior door. It was still dark enough outside that they hoped that they could leave undetected. Destiny peaked out the door. The pasture was quiet. She could see a few cows laying down sleeping. She could not see the neighbor's house or the barn.

Famous came up behind her and nervously asked, "See anything?"

"Cows. I'm going to sneak a peek." Destiny walked out the door and Famous followed. They kept their backs against the wall and inched their way to the corner. Destiny slowly looked around the corner. She still couldn't see anything. Destiny went around the corner and continued down the next side of the pumphouse. Famous followed. She looked around the next corner, but the barn was blocking her view of the house. She turned back and told Famous.

Famous turned to see that Darla and Angelica were behind her. She whispered to them about the barn. Angelica looked around to get her bearings and decide the best path to get out of the pasture. They were supposed to meet someone who agreed to take the girls to the west coast. It wasn't far if they could get to the road. They had a chance to make it.

Angelica pulled Destiny's sleeve and waved her to turn back and come to her. "I think the best plan is to get to the road," she advised. "It's still early. I doubt they are even up, but you and Famous should run for it. I'm not sure if I can. When you get to the road, go to town. Go to the alley behind the café. Your second cousin will be there to take you to the coast."

"What about you and mom?" Destiny asked.

"You know we have our ways. Don't worry about us. Just call us and let us know you're safe. Do you have your phone?"

"I put it in my backpack when I went to bed." The four of them hugged each other tightly. Destiny turned to Famous. "Ready, Famous?"

"I'll follow you," she answered.

Destiny and Famous ran through the pasture toward the road. Famous glanced back at the house. It was dark and she could see no sign of life, so she slowed to a jog. "Destiny, I don't think anyone is up. I think we're okay."

"It doesn't matter. Are you forgetting we are in the open and basically trespassing? We need to move and move fast." Destiny called back to her.

Just then, they thought they heard a shot. Maybe it was only thunder. Glancing back, Destiny could see Famous running behind her. Destiny tripped and tumbled to the ground. She laid their until Famous caught up to her.

"Are you okay?" Famous asked, grabbing her hand and helping her up. She looked at the pumphouse and could see that her grandmother and Aunt Darla were gone. The house now had lights on, and an exceptionally large man was walking in their direction, gun in hand.

"We gotta go!" Famous yelled and nodded in the man's direction. Destiny looked back and they took off running. They could hear him yelling to get off his property. Famous was sure she wanted off his property more than he did.

They ran and ran. Looking back again, they saw they had put a lot of distance between themselves and the man. He looked to be labored and walking slow. They heard the sound of a car passing by.

"We're almost to the road," Destiny was breathing heavily as the words came from her mouth. The road was finally in their sight. They came to a fence. Luckily, the fence wasn't electric, but it had barbed wire. They took turns holding up a line of wire for the other to crawl through.

CHAPTER TWENTY-SIX

Julia Never Shuts Up

Town and the café were only a short distance. A police car slowed as it passed them walking on the road.

"No doubt he called the police," said Destiny. "We can cut through the cemetery and get off the road."

They walked in silence. After a while, Famous asked, "Did you hear a gunshot?"

"I'm not sure," Destiny answered.

"What's the bad blood with the neighbor about?"

"After Mawmaw sold them the property, they held a summoning of some kind causing the ground to shake. There was a storm. Lightning struck the barn, and it burned to the ground."

"How could they blame Mawmaw?"

"There's more to it, but now is not the time. There's the café."

They walked to the alley and a car was waiting there. The person inside was looking at their phone and didn't notice them walk up. Destiny tapped on the window.

A girl rolled the window down. "Get in!" she smiled. They climbed in the car and the girl quickly drove out of the alley. "I had almost given up on you. I'm guessing you're Famous. Sorry I didn't make it yesterday. I was at work. I'm Julia, your second cousin."

Julia was driving fast. "Nice to meet you, are we in a hurry?" Famous asked

"As a matter of fact, we are! I have to get you two to Galway and it's over two hours away. If we're late you'll be stuck. I'm sure Angelica told you, right?" She kept on talking without waiting for an answer. "Wow, you two sure do look like twins. I mean, I was told you looked like twins, but I thought it was an exaggeration. You know, like when someone says another person is practically their twin and you see them and you're like 'I don't see it…' Anyway, so as I was saying, we have a cousin who knows someone that owns a fishing boat that is heading to Iceland. Usually they leave out at the crack of dawn, but they're waiting on a shipment or something. So—"

"Take a breath, Julia," Destiny interrupted. "You never stop talking. Mawmaw never told us about the travel arrangements. We had quite a night."

Destiny told Julia about the storm and tunnel and the neighbor. Famous thought that she probably shouldn't have mentioned the tunnel, but the cat was out of the bag before she could stop her.

Julia drove like she was being chased by the police. Famous looked out the back window and was happy to see that there were no other cars behind them. She took out her map. "Destiny how do I work this thing?"

"Just put your thumb on the corner where the compass is."

Famous did as she was told and watched as it appeared to unfold into its original size. She looked at the map. "I don't understand this." She showed the map to Destiny, but Destiny was in the front seat and couldn't see it well enough. "Here, take it and look at it." Famous tried to hand it to her.

"Famous, the second you take your hand off it the map will disappear. Just wait until we get to Galway."

Famous studied the map for several minutes. She could see two lines: one to Galway and one to Derry. "But there are two lines. Maybe we're supposed to follow the other line and go to Derry."

Julia looked at Famous in the rearview mirror. "Listen, it doesn't matter. I'm taking you to Galway."

"But there's a skull-and-crossbones symbol—"

"Famous just put it away," Destiny interrupted. "It will drive you crazy! When I first got mine, I saw stuff like that and it freaked me out. I didn't want to leave the house. If it makes you feel better, I'll look at mine in a bit. The main thing is to get to the book."

"What if the book is moved?"

"Your map will lead us to the book even if it's moved. As long as one of those lines leads us to Galway, we are on track. Sometimes the journey changes, but the destination remains the same. It's just giving you options, and trust me, there is no option without some kind of warning."

Julia continued to drive as fast as she could manage. She babbled about her work and the last time she had seen Destiny. She brought up the fact they looked so much alike again. Famous drowned her out after a while thinking she talked way too much, especially considering how crazy she was driving.

Famous looked out the back window again. She saw a car crest the hill behind them and immediately got nervous. She watched until it went out of sight when they turned on a curve in the road. Once in a while she would catch a glimpse of it far in the distance. She just wanted the ride to be over. They pulled into the port just as the boat was loading several crates onto the stern.

"There it is," Julia said. She barely had the car in park before bolting out to talk to the man standing next to the boat. Julia waved them out of the car and over to the man. The man instructed the girls to go aboard the boat, down below, and to make themselves comfortable. They said goodbye to Julia and thanked her for the ride. Julia left as quickly as she had gotten there.

CHAPTER TWENTY-SEVEN

AND WE'RE OFF

Famous walked down the stairs leading to the salon. A couple of guys walked through. She thought must be crew members or fishermen. They nodded and smiled but didn't stop for a conversation.

Destiny walked through toward the bow. It was a little messy, but not filthy. She glanced in the galley and saw a few dishes in the sink, a corkboard on the wall that had papers tacked in place, and a map with several pins in it.

Suddenly, the engines roared to life. Destiny made her way back to Famous. A man Famous was sure was the captain came below and told them to stay there until they were out of the port. They sat on a couch silently. The men were yelling back and forth about releasing lines.

"I can't believe we're doing this. It's completely crazy," Famous whispered to Destiny.

"I know," Destiny replied.

"I'm totally freaked out right now." Famous could feel a slight warmth coming from the amulets. She wondered what it could mean.

"Me, too." Destiny grabbed Famous's hand. "But I'm sure we'll be fine."

The man came down below again saying, "And we're off! I'm the captain, Captain Nick. You can call me Cap or Nick… whatever. It's not my business, but are you two running from the law? I only ask in case we see the Coast Guard or something."

"No way, seriously? You thought we were fugitives?" Famous was laughing. "Us?"

"Well it's not often I get a call in the middle of the night asking me to stow away a couple beautiful twins," he replied with a chuckle.

"Oh, we're not twins," Destiny said with her Irish accent.

"You don't sound the same, but—" Another man came down and whispered something in the captain's ear. "Are you expecting company?"

"No, why?"

"Stay here!"

Captain Nick followed the other man up onto the deck. The girls could hear him shouting back and forth to someone in the pilot house. Moments later, he reappeared.

"Seems somebody is looking for you two. Don't worry, I was clear with the crew. No one knows you're on this boat. Do you at least have passports?"

Famous was the first to speak. "I do!" she exclaimed proudly. The man looked at Destiny and she shook her head.

"What?" Famous asked, eyes growing wide. "How are you planning to get back into Ireland, Destiny? Everyone I know from Europe has one."

"I have one, just not with me," she replied. "I can have my mom overnight it to me."

"To where? The Atlantic Ocean?" Famous asked sarcastically.

"Don't yell at me, Famous!" Destiny laughed.

The captain was watching the girls spat when he asked, "Famous for what?"

"That's her name—Famous."

"Your names are Famous and Destiny? That's a little different. Okay, well, Famous and Destiny, we have a few days to figure it out. I have an idea so let's just not worry about it now. Are you two hungry? Because I'm starved and I'm sure the guys could eat. Either of you know how to cook?" The girls nodded.

The boat rolled over a wave, rocking the girls in their seats. Nick caught Destiny before she hit the floor. "Thanks," she smiled as she steadied herself. She and Famous walked to the galley. The captain went up to the pilot house.

The boat rocked back and forth. Famous and Destiny attempted to figure out some kind of a meal. They found stuff to make sandwiches. Famous took out the butter, ham, cheese, and a tomato. "How many guys are out there?" she asked.

"I'll check," Destiny answered. She took the stairs up and looked around the boat. The land was only slightly visible through a hazy mist. Nick saw her from the pilot house and waved her up. She was thinking of how exciting it was that she was out on the high seas. She walked into the pilothouse. "I'm just checking on how many crewmen are aboard."

"Just three of us," he told her. "So, what kind of trouble are you and your sister in?"

"We're not sisters, just cousins, and we aren't really in trouble, so to speak. It's a long story."

"Well, we have days, so go ahead."

"Maybe later. As I said, I came up for a headcount for lunch." Destiny darted out the door before he could say anything. She went back to Famous and told her how many were aboard. Destiny warmed some soup while Famous grilled sandwiches. Two of the guys came down to eat and Famous took the captain his food.

"Which one are you?" he asked.

"Famous," she answered.

He made a mental note that Famous is American. Her hair was slightly less auburn but not overly noticeable unless they are standing next to each other.

"Destiny said you are cousins," he stated. He took a bite of the sandwich. "Good sandwich. Thanks. Who's chasing you?"

"Why do you think someone is chasing us?" Famous was uncomfortable and felt a little heat from the amulets again. It made her think maybe it's not the amulets as much as it is her feeling threatened or worried.

"That call on the radio when we were leaving port. Someone asked them to hail me and ask if I had a woman on board. I told them to say no we do not have *a* woman on board, which is technically true."

"Really, did they say who was asking?"

"Nope!"

Famous was thinking that whoever it is doesn't know there are two of them. She had to tell Destiny. "I'm going to go eat. See you later." She ran out and ran smack into one of the other guys. "I'm sorry."

"No running on deck!" he yelled sternly.

"Oh, of course. I won't, umm, run." Famous's voice was shaking. She continued past him quickly. She couldn't wait to tell Destiny what she had heard. They could definitely use this to their advantage.

When Famous got back to the galley, Destiny was in a conversation with the other crewman. She didn't want to say anything in front of him so she sat down at the table to eat her sandwich and soup and wait to be alone with Destiny.

It seemed like forever when the captain came in and told the crewman to hit the rack so he could take some of the night watch. He walked out of the galley but stood by the door to listen to them talk without them knowing.

"Destiny, great news. I talked to the captain and when we were leaving port, they asked him if he had a woman on board. *A* woman. Not *two* women. Whoever was asking doesn't know we're together."

"Okay… and this is great news, because?" Destiny asked, chewing a bite of her sandwich.

"Don't you see? They don't know there are two of us. We could use that to our advantage."

The captain walked back in the room. "Ladies, I think you have some explaining to do. I just got hailed again by the Coast Guard asking questions about my crew. I need to know what's going on and now!" he demanded.

Famous and Destiny looked at each other, then at Nick. Famous began by saying, "It's complicated, and I'm pretty sure you won't believe a word of it."

"Try me," he replied.

Destiny cut in before Famous could say anything. "Let's just give him the short version, shall we? We are trying to locate a stolen artifact while the one, or ones, chasing us are trying to stop us. They are willing to do anything to stop us, even harm us. Well, to stop Famous. We don't think they know about me. We have done nothing illegal. Only thing is, I don't have my passport and that sucks, but we're moving on."

"Hmm…" He stood there looking at them trying to decide if he believed their story.

"We hoped that we would be able to get away from Ireland undetected because we're in extreme danger," added Famous.

"I think what Famous is saying is we really appreciate you sticking your neck out there to help a couple of damsels in distress," said Destiny.

"Yes, that is exactly what I was about to say. What exactly did the Coast Guard say?"

"Oh, I lied about that," he replied.

CHAPTER TWENTY-EIGHT

HOW LONG DOES IT TAKE TO GET TO ICELAND?

"Really?" Destiny asked him begrudgingly. "Are you freaking kidding me? I was totally out of my mind. I was trying to figure out where to hide. I mean, Famous would be fine, but I don't know. What would they do to me with no passport?"

"You must have some kind of ID. You just can't leave the boat unless we are in an Irish port. Besides, I've never smuggled anyone to another country so I needed to know what was going on. What's the artifact and who stole it?"

"It's a rare—well, actually, a one-of-a-kind, book," Destiny said, trying to make it sound important.

"You're risking your life for a book?" He looked shocked. "And you know it's in Iceland, how?"

Destiny looked at Famous. "It's—"

"I know, I know, a long story." Nick shook his head.

"It really is a long story, but we think it's actually in Greenland. We won't know until we get to Iceland." Famous was annoyed that Destiny was spilling her guts to this guy.

"How do you plan to get to Greenland?" The whole story had piqued his interest and he thought about the spy movies he liked to watch.

"Not a clue," Famous replied.

"Famous, we will figure it out," Destiny assured her, sitting back down at the table to finish her food.

Suddenly, Famous felt like she had lost all gravity as the boat was hit by a massive wave. She flew across the galley, then hit the wall and crumbled to the floor.

The captain tried to catch her but lost his footing and landed on the table. The boat was still crashing through waves. Famous tried to get up but could only manage to crawl to the table and climb up on the booth next to Destiny. She asked Famous if she was okay and said she was.

The captain immediately went to the pilothouse after he regained his footing. The weather had become treacherous with no warning. The wind was blowing. He couldn't tell if it was sleet or the ocean closing in on them. The sky had turned dark as night. The crew member that had hit his rack a little while ago brought them lifejackets. "Here, you should put these on," he told them. Destiny was too frightened to move. Famous helped her put hers on after she had clicked the last buckle of her own.

The boat had rocked back and forth for what seemed like hours before the ocean grew calm. Once they were sure the storm was over, the girls decided to get some air. When they climbed the stairs and opened the door, a burst of cold air hit them.

It was so cold Famous could see her breath. She wrapped her arm around Destiny as she shivered. They stood on the deck watching the waves. They looked back and could see the three guys talking.

"How long does it take to get Iceland?" Famous asked.

"Good question! You should go ask the captain," answered Destiny. She looked back at the men. "I kind of wish we had checked that out before we got on the boat."

"Me, too, but there wasn't exactly time." Famous looked out into the vast sea. "What are we going to do when we get there?"

"Check out the map. We may even have to try to take another trip inside the map."

"Can we do that?"

"I think so. Actually, I have no idea, Famous."

"We should check out the map now. We have nothing but time. I'll go ask our ETA and then we'll check it out. We should compare yours to mine. What do you think?" Famous didn't wait for her to answer before she ran off to talk to the captain. It thrilled her to think about comparing maps.

Famous talked to the captain and ran back to find Destiny. She found her inside cleaning the galley. Soup had gone everywhere when the wave hit. Famous picked up a bowl from the floor and helped Destiny clean up the mess.

After they finished cleaning the galley, Famous urged Destiny to get her map. They went to the salon, grabbed their backpacks, and sat on the couch. Famous fished out her map and Destiny did the same. They opened them at the same time. The line on Destiny's was the same as Famous's, but unexpectedly stopped at Iceland.

Famous took the amulets out of her pocket. "Maybe these will help." She closed her eyes and squeezed the amulets, "Show me where the *Book of Wisdom* is," she ordered the amulets. She focused all of her energy and concentration on the amulets. They glowed brightly enough to light the room.

Destiny watched as Famous's map began to illuminate a vision of the book in the western part of Iceland.

"Famous look!" Destiny exclaimed.

Famous opened her eyes to see the vision. "I thought it was in Greenland. I guess I was wrong. I mean, it was so far away and hard to read under the circumstances."

"I couldn't see it at all because it was so far. Maybe it was in Greenland, but person that has it is on the move. Let's just hope we get there before they leave Iceland. When did the captain say that will that be?"

"Four days."

"Yikes!"

"Yeah, yikes." Famous looked at the map for a few minutes. "It looks like we take a different path right here. Then, look at that!" She pointed to a picture on the map. "What's that symbol mean?"

"Look at the legend on the bottom."

"I did, it's not there."

Destiny leaned over and looked at the symbol and the legend. "I told you not to pay attention to it. It will drive you loony because next time you look at it, everything will be completely different." She took her thumb off her map and put it away.

Famous stared at hers for a few more minutes. "It reminds me of a funnel or like—"

"Just let it go, Famous!"

"Fine!" She put her map away but was obviously annoyed about it. "You know, you've had a lot more time to adjust than I have."

Destiny hugged Famous apologetically. "I know. I'm trying to save you from some of the frustration I went through."

CHAPTER TWENTY-NINE

FINALLY

The days seemed to pass slowly and yet quickly at the same time. Famous and Destiny spent the time really getting to know each other. They talked about their childhood and their life before Famous started her journey and before the day they had met at the bus stop.

They played cards with the crew members, Todd and Joel. Even the captain joined in on a game or two. They learned how to steer the boat and each caught several fish. It was a true bonding experience. Famous wrote each day in her journal and shared her mom's journal with Destiny.

On the last day, Famous and Destiny were fixing lunch when they heard one of the men announce they were approaching land. They darted out on to the deck to see land in the distance.

"Finally!" Famous exclaimed.

"It hasn't been so bad, has it?" Destiny asked.

Famous hugged her. "No, not at all. It's been amazing."

They watched nervously as they got closer to land. The captain yelled down to them to go inside when they were nearly at the port. Down below, Destiny paced back and forth. Famous kept telling her they would be okay. Nick had a plan and it sounded pretty solid. As soon as they arrived at a marina Nick went ashore and checked them in. He had to take all of their passports with him.

He knew if he could check in without being boarded, they would be in the clear. He had brought supplies from Ireland several times and had his cargo inspected a lot of them but had only been boarded once. He felt confident.

The office was so busy that he had to wait several minutes. After registering their passports, he waited to hear if they were going to come inspect his cargo. He recognized the inspecting agent, who had come out of his office to meet with him. The man smiled and obviously recognized him, too.

"Mr. Nick, so good to see you again," the man said.

"Jon, how's the family?" Nick asked. They shook hands and chatted for a few minutes. Nick told them that they would be there for only a day or two and Jon sent him on his way.

Nick made his way back to the boat. He boarded and went into the salon. Famous asked how it went. He told her it was all good. Then, he asked where Destiny was.

"She's hiding," Famous laughed. "Destiny, it's cool. You can come out."

Nick explained how it was going to work. He had use of a truck to deliver supplies. He would take Famous somewhere and drop her off. Keeping her passport then come back load the truck and take Destiny to famous. That way if they got stopped on the way out for a passport check, they would be covered.

Famous was not excited about separating with Destiny or not having her passport, but it seemed like the only way. Destiny was nervous about it as well and Famous could tell. She hugged her and told her it would be fine.

Famous and Nick left to get the truck while the crew unloaded the cargo. The truck was waiting in the parking lot. It was an older model from the eighties, she guessed. It was blue and obviously a work truck with plenty of rust spots. He got in and started it up. Famous climbed in the passenger seat.

"There's a couple of restaurants close by where you can get some coffee or something," he told her. He slowed as he left the marina, then pulled out on the main road. "Well, lucky for us no one is checking passports today." He drove for about five minutes and came to a café. "Okay, it will be a while because I have to load up."

Famous thanked him as she got out of the truck.

"Good luck and be safe, Famous," he said. She smiled, thanked him again, and closed the door. Famous wandered into the café and was surprised that they spoke English when she was shown to a table. She sat down, ordered coffee, and waited for Destiny.

Time ticked by slowly. Famous was getting fidgety. She tried not to look at the clock ticking on the wall. Many questions ran through her mind. What would she do if he didn't bring Destiny? What if they got stopped? What if they asked Destiny questions and she didn't know the correct answers? Then, there was the Irish accent with a US passport.

The amulets were warming in her pocket. Now she was wondering if it was a warning or her own anxiety. The server offered more coffee just as Destiny walked in. Famous let out a sigh of relief. "Finally," she said and asked for another cup for Destiny.

Destiny sat with Famous and waited for her coffee. They ordered something to eat and talked casually about how nervous they had been when they left the marina. Destiny told Famous that Nick knew the guy in the office, so they had gotten lucky.

CHAPTER THIRTY

LET'S DO THIS!

"I can't believe we are in Iceland. This is so cool!" Destiny exclaimed with excitement.

"If only it were a vacation. I need to figure out where we go from here," Famous responded. They stopped talking when the server walked up to place their plates in front of them. Famous continued after the server was out of earshot. "Then, we will have to figure out how we are going to get you out of the country without a passport. I guess we should have asked Nick if he could give us a ride back to Ireland once we find the book. I didn't really think about it because that's in the opposite direction of the forest."

Destiny's excitement faded a little wondering if Famous wanted to go on without her after they found the book. She shook her head and perked back up. "Well, we're here now and we'll find the *Book of Wisdom* and figure it out from there. One step at a time! Now let's go and find that book, Famous."

Famous paid the bill and off they went. She needed to look at the map. She had wanted to look at it in the restaurant, but the place was packed.

"It might be early enough to find the book today, but we know we'll be here for at least one night," Famous told Destiny. "I think we should get a hotel, drop off our backpacks, study the map, and make a plan."

"Let's do this," Destiny agreed.

They made their way to a hotel, got checked in, and went to their room. The room had two twin beds, a small sofa, and a table with two chairs. It was a rather plain room, but it met their needs.

Famous sat at the table, took out her map and opened it. She noticed the map had changed to only show Iceland. The path led her to the lava tunnels and crystal caves. Destiny looked over her shoulder and then pulled out her own map. They were elated her path was the same.

Famous made a few phone inquiries about finding transportation to the lava tunnel. There was a round trip tour available and they could make it if they hurried. She put her map in her pocket along with her passport, credit card, and other ID. She emptied her clothes on the bed.

Famous noticed a book that she hadn't packed. Picking it up and looking at it, she thought Angelica or Darla must have put it in her backpack. There was no time to think about that because they needed to get going so she put the book aside. She grabbed the empty backpack to carry the *Book of Wisdom* back in if they found it. She had emptied it in case she needed to run and didn't want the extra weight. Destiny grabbed her ID but left her backpack behind.

Famous had picked a hotel that they could come and go from their room without dealing with a lobby or elevators. She pulled on the hood of her coat and carefully looked out the door of the room. The amulets had been fluctuating in temperature all day—hot, then cold, then hot, then cold again. It made her feel somewhat uneasy. She waved to Destiny to follow her and they quickly walked to meet the tour bus.

Destiny also pulled on her hood. It was as much to hide their face as it was to stay warm. The temperature was getting colder as the day wore on. They made their way to the tour bus. Famous bought two warm scarves along the way at a shop. She wrapped one around Destiny covering half her face. Then wrapped her own the same way. They joined the line that was formed at the tour bus stop.

Destiny and Famous chatted about the tour. They were super excited. Unexpectedly, a strange feeling came over Famous. She stopped mid-sentence and looked around.

"What is it?" Destiny whispered as her eyes followed Famous's. Nothing appeared to be wrong, but she began to feel nervous. Again, she asked Famous what was going on.

"I don't know," Famous whispered back. "I have this strange feeling someone is watching us." She looked around again, but no one appeared to even notice them. The tour bus driver gave them the spiel about the lava tunnel—it was an unguided tour, there was a specific amount of time for the whole excursion, explained the equipment, etcetera.

The girls climbed on board the bus. Famous sat near the window at first, but Destiny begged her for the window seat so she traded. Famous could not get over the feeling that something wasn't right. The bus engine came to life, the door closed, and they began their journey to the caves to find the *Book of Wisdom*.

The trip took less than an hour. When they arrive, the tourists disembarked the bus in anticipation. Famous and Destiny followed the crowd and geared up to go into the caves. Everyone moved toward the tunnels. Near the entrance, the girls slowed their pace allowing some distance to separate them from the others. Famous needed to be sure that they were not being followed. Famous looked around for a place that would give her and Destiny some privacy.

Famous hid in a dark area away from the others with Destiny standing in front of her to block her from view. Famous shoved her hand in her pocket and squeezed the amulets. She concentrated on the book. She tried to hide the glow of the amulets, visualizing the book in her mind. She could see it. It was surrounded by darkness and a shadow hovered over it.

Destiny could see a figure out of her peripheral vision. She looked in the direction of the figure but saw only darkness. The glow from behind her was getting brighter and brighter. Destiny could hear the tourists murmuring.

Famous could hear a voice whisper, "Don't panic, Famous." It was familiar to her, but she couldn't place it. She continued to look for distinguishing marks in the darkness that surrounded the book.

The whispering continued, "Don't panic, Famous... the crystal... don't fall... don't panic." The repeated whispers were confusing and forced Famous to lose sight of the book and see a blue haze of crystals. She tried to break the vision, but one crystal shined the brightest. It glowed a purplish-blue light.

Destiny tried to get Famous's attention, but she seemed to be in a trance. The glow behind her was nearly blinding and Destiny could hear the other tourists getting closer. Destiny grabbed Famous and shook her. The light faded to darkness just as a member of the group came into view. Destiny held her flashlight toward them only moving it when they covered their eyes.

Destiny grabbed Famous's arm and walked her deeper into the tunnel. When they were far enough away from the group, Destiny spoke. "What happened, did you see the book?" Famous told her about her vision. The vision confused them, and it didn't give them the direction they were hoping for.

"I don't think the book is here," Famous said. "I can't explain it, but I feel like I need to find the crystal that was in my vision." She was walking around looking at the walls of the cave. She felt pulled in a particular direction that was not part of the tour.

Destiny followed her and watched as she touched the wall. A flicker of blue light streaked across the cavern and into a dark cave-like area. Famous ran to follow the light until she came to what seemed like the end of the cave. It was dark and damp. She was feeling around the wall and saw small flickers of lights appear.

Destiny caught up to her, the beam of her flashlight bounced off the wall. Famous told Destiny that she felt drawn to this place. It had called to her. Destiny told her to ask the amulets.

Famous held them in her hand and said the words aloud, "Help me to understand why I am here." Suddenly the ground shook, it felt like an earthquake. Destiny immediately thought about the volcanic eruptions she had read about earlier in the brochures about the lava tunnels.

Rocks tumbled from the wall, it seemed as if the earth was going to split in half. Destiny had lost her balance, slipped, and fell backwards. A minute or two seemed like an eternity. Screams and voices could be heard a distance away. Suddenly it all came to a stop, Destiny was sitting on the ground, she reached over, and picked up her flashlight.

Famous caught her breath as the picture in her vision appeared in front of her. She touched the crystalized wall. Her eyes drifted down to the brightest place on the wall. She reached out and the crystal came to her. She turned, opened her hand, and showed the crystal to Destiny. "This is why I am here."

Famous shoved the crystal and amulets into her pocket, grabbed Destiny's hand, and pulled her up off the ground. They quickly ran through the tunnel to join the group that had gathered outside. The tour bus driver counted the tourists as they came out. They were the last two on the list.

The driver had been on the phone reporting the event before he ushered the guests back on the bus. He started the engine and turned back toward the city. Destiny and Famous sat quietly listening to the excited voices chattering about the earthquake, some calling it an eruption. Famous couldn't help imagining how exaggerated the story would become by the time they reached their destination.

CHAPTER THIRTY-ONE

WITCHCRAFT 101

Back at the hotel, Famous ordered a pizza and some sodas. She pulled out the crystal and set it on the bed next to her map and the amulets. Destiny flipped on the TV for noise, then went in to take a much-needed hot shower to warm her bones.

Famous stared at the crystal, light danced around the room as she held it up. It appeared clear, then blue, then purple. She was mesmerized by it and felt like it was a part of her or belonged to her.

"It's your thing, isn't it?" Destiny's voice startled her.

"Huh?" Famous asked.

"Remember when we talked about the amulets and my medallion? Every witch has a thing—a lucky charm, a conduit to enhance their power." Destiny was about to continue on when they heard a knock on the door. She peered out the small peephole in the door before answering. It was the pizza they'd ordered.

Destiny placed the pizza box on the table. She flipped it open and breathed in the heavenly scent. Famous was quick to join her at the table. They mindlessly watched the TV as they ate, their earlier conversation forgotten.

Famous groaned as she got up and grabbed her stomach. "Why did I eat so much?" she moaned. She wandered over to lay down on her bed. Destiny decided that looked like a great idea and laid down as well. The girls quickly fell asleep.

Famous had strange dreams of the crystal beaming her into space. She was floating high above the earth. She could see Destiny far below reaching up to her. When their hands touched, she fell from the heavens and then they were running in the forest.

She kept asking herself how she got in the forest. Then, she heard the whispering voice she'd heard in the tunnel. "Don't panic, Famous… realize you're not dreaming… don't fall." It was confusing. The crystal was in her hand and then she was floating again. A noise from the TV startled her awake. Her eyes fluttered open and she fell to the floor.

The loud thud awoke Destiny. She saw Famous sitting on the floor. "What are you doing, Famous?"

"I'm not sure." Famous stood up and sat next to Destiny on her bed. She told her of her dream. "I think I was floating around the room." She still had the crystal in her hand. "Is that possible? I mean—"

"Oh, it's totally possible Famous!" Destiny exclaimed excitedly. "You probably transported! I personally haven't tried, but lots of witches have told stories about transporting to other places."

Destiny regaled Famous with story after story that she had been told about witches transporting themselves to different places. Then, Famous thought of several times their grandmother had seemed to appear and disappear.

"Maybe, just maybe, this is how we get to the book," Famous announced grinning. "And I think it is a brilliant way to get you out of

Iceland without a passport. What do you think? Are you in?"

"I have always wanted to really take my magic for a spin, but you know Mawmaw and Mom always stopped me. They seemed to always know what I was up to before I even did it." Destiny sat for a minute. "I'm definitely in!"

"Okay, but how do we do it?"

Destiny shrugged. "That is the question, isn't it?"

Famous felt exhilarated by the possibility. She knew she would never be able to go back to sleep. She jumped up and started some coffee. She and Destiny talked for hours about her dream, the whispers, the lava tunnel, and their lucky charms. They discussed their ideas about how to transport but really had no idea. They laughed about needing a witchcraft 101 course.

"I just don't get it. You were around it your whole life, right?" Famous poured the last of the coffee into their cups.

"There is a big difference in being around it and using it. I've basically used the parlor trick version of magic," Destiny chuckled. "If only we had the book, it would tell us."

Famous started laughing. "It would tell us how to beam ourselves to itself." She stopped laughing an. thought for a minute. "Wait, he book. You're brilliant! The book!" Destiny looked confused as Famous ran over to the clothes she had piled on the chair in the corner. Digging to the bottom of the pile she pulled out the book and showed Destiny.

"*The Mystery of Witches and Magic Spells.*" Destiny read the title aloud. "Where'd you get that?"

"I found it in my backpack today when I dumped it out," Famous replied. "Angelica or your mom must have put it there." Famous opened to the table of contents. "Ready to get a little witchcraft 101?"

"Definitely!"

Famous read the introduction out loud. Destiny held on to every word. Most of it sounded like pure fiction, which reminded Famous of what Angelica had said about it. She read through the chapter titles. "This seems kind of… what's the word I'm looking for?"

"Stupid?" Destiny said with a chuckle. "Maybe there's something useful. Let me see."

Destiny flipped to the index in the back. "How about this section on crystals?" Destiny flipped to the page indicated in the index and read it aloud.

Crystals can be helpful in many spells, often giving the spell caster sight into past and future events. It is said certain crystals can belong to certain witches, but it is unproven. It is believed that the right crystals are rarely found by the right witches. In the rare circumstance it happens, the power of the crystal and the witch's gift are multiplied. Of course, this is only what is written, not proven. The following pages will illustrate spells that are most effective with crystals.

Famous looked at her crystal laying on the table. "Sounds kind of crazy, you have to admit it. You know what Angelica said about this book, right?"

"Yeah. It's mostly fiction, but it won't hurt to give it a read. You have to admit what happened at the lava tunnels would have sounded pretty crazy, too. Yet, we know it happened. Maybe I can find something useful for us. We have some time to kill before anything opens. Also, I better call home. I should have days ago, I bet my mom and our grandmother are worried about us."

Famous got up, walked to the table, and picked up the crystal. "While you read that, I'm going to take a shower. Then, we will check the maps again and figure out our next plan. I'm starting to wonder if this—" she held up the crystal, "—is the reason we are here in Iceland. Not the book."

"But Mawmaw said—"

Famous interrupted, "It seems like no one really knows for sure. Everyone is going by what they've been told. Basically, it's like what you said about the amulets. It's like that book you're holding. It's what's written but not proven. We don't even know who has actually read the *Book of Wisdom*." Famous walked into the bathroom and turned on the water.

CHAPTER THIRTY-TWO

WHAT IF?

Destiny read through the pages of spells with crystals, then the spells with other various charms, potions, and varying degrees of gifts or powers in witches, warlocks, and wizards. She came to a page that had been highlighted. It mentioned using a charm to get to your destination on the map. She read it several times but couldn't totally make sense of it.

She heard the shower shut off and called out, "Famous, I think I found something."

Famous came out of the bathroom wearing a bathrobe and her hair wrapped in a towel. "What is it?" she asked. Famous walked over to see what Destiny was talking about and Destiny handed her the book.

"You see that? It's highlighted. I bet Mawmaw did that." She pointed to the page. "I don't really understand the instructions."

Famous read the words out loud.

"Travel here, travel there, you may travel anywhere. Map a spot and please beware. Use your charm without alarm. Hold your destination in your hand and heart. Think of nothing else or you'll be torn apart."

"It is a little cryptic, but I think we can figure it out. Although, that last part is kind of scary," Famous said. She read the words again. "Hmm, I think before we go trying anything, you should call home. Also check out the map again."

"Good idea!" Destiny called her mom, but there was no answer. She called their grandmother who answered on the very first ring. Angelica scolded her for making them worry. Then, she listened to the long story of what had happened since they left her at the pumphouse.

Listening to Destiny talk to their grandmother, a thought jumped into Famous's mind about that day. Angelica and Darla were standing at the pumphouse when they ran but were gone the next time she looked back. She remembered Angelica saying something about not going back through the tunnel, which really only leaves a couple of other possibilities—they either walked above-ground or transported.

Destiny was listening on the phone and occasionally answering. Famous nudged Destiny and kept whispering for her to ask her about the spell in the book. Destiny held up her hand and told her to hold on. Finally, Destiny held the phone out to Famous, "She wants to talk to you."

"Me? Why?" Famous asked. Destiny shrugged as she held the phone out for her. Famous took the phone, "Hello?"

Angelica told Famous to check her map before trying any crazy spell in that book. She was sorry she had even sent it with her after she really had time to think about it. She told her some stories about the dangers of getting trapped or suspended in time. She finished up by telling her that it is a terrible idea to mess with those kinds of spells when you don't know what you're doing.

Famous listened to her and felt her heart skip a beat when she mentioned being trapped. She knew all too well about being trapped. She had been trapped after lifting a curse. Finally,

Famous asked her, "So, what do we do about Destiny's passport? Because I'm not sure the *Book of Wisdom* is actually here." There was a long silence on the phone. "Hello? Did I lose you? Are you there?"

"Yes, I'm here. I'm just thinking," Angelica replied. "Well your goal is to get the book, so follow your map. It will take you on the path you need to take to accomplish that goal. Only use magic or spells as the absolute last possible resort."

They said their goodbyes and Famous hung up feeling frustrated. Part of her was ready for this adventure to be over. She thought about home. How long had it been since she had been home? She felt like it had been a decade.

Destiny set her map on the table and Famous walked over to see what direction the path went. "Well, that's weird. What do you make of that?" Famous asked as she pulled her own map out to compare. It was the same as Destiny's map.

"Maybe I should call Mawmaw back," Destiny offered.

"I don't know. What could it possibly mean when there is no path, but there's a destination?"

Destiny paced around the room thinking. "I think I know what it means." She grabbed the book from the bed. She ran her fingers across the lettering on the front and mindlessly read them, *"The Mysteries of Witches and Magic Spells."* She flipped it open to the page they had read many times that morning. Out of curiosity she turned to the next page and read it to herself.

This riddle was said to come from an ancient journal of a wizard. It is said that if you hold a picture or map and your charm and focus only on that destination and read the spell or say the words, you can travel to that location without losing time. But if your thoughts waiver even a little you can be ripped from your time or possibly be trapped in another time or space.

Destiny flipped to the next page and it was blank. She flipped to the next and the next. The way she was frantically flipping the pages caught Famous's attention. "What's up Destiny?"

"I'm looking for the spell." She continued to flip through the pages, then turned to Famous. "Here, read this." She turned back to the page about the riddle and handed Famous the book. Famous read it and did the same as Destiny flipping through the pages looking for the spell.

A knock on the door startled them both. Famous looked out the peephole to see the housekeeper standing there. She looked at her watch and opened the door. Famous thought that it was odd because it wasn't quite checkout time.

The housekeeper was checking to see if they needed her to make up the room or if they were going to be checking out. Famous told her they hadn't decided if they were checking out or staying another night. The housekeeper said that if they were leaving, they could leave the key in the room. Famous thanked her.

"We have about two hours until checkout time to make a decision, Destiny. We are running out of time." Destiny had been reading through the spells again. She could not find any that referenced the riddle or the wizards' journal. "Should I ring up the office and extend another night?" Famous asked. Destiny hadn't heard her. She was too engrossed in the book. Famous raised her voice a little to get Destiny's attention. "Destiny!" Destiny looked up from the book. "I asked if you thought I should ring up the office and extend another night?"

Destiny looked at the time. "I'm thinking let's wait until we absolutely have to. Maybe we can figure this out. I've been thinking. There is no path on the map, only a destination. I think it's a sign that we have to try to find this spell." Destiny took her medallion off her neck and touched the blank page in the book. "Show me the spell to travel."

They watched as nothing happened. Famous pulled the amulets from her pocket, "Here, try these too." She set them in Destiny's hand.

"I've never used the amulets, maybe you should—" They began to glow and Destiny looked at them.

"They're glowing. I don't understand how they work, but usually they start feeling—"

"Hot!"

"Yeah, hot. But I haven't figured out if they are actually hot or if it's just a sensation in my skin. Sometimes I think I'm controlling them when I get scared or nervous. Then, all of a sudden, they will feel hot in my pocket for no reason and I think it's warning me of some impending doom." Famous giggled at her own confusion.

"Maybe they do all of those things," Destiny suggested, holding them in her hand and noticing they were no longer glowing. She squeezed them. "How did they work when you lifted the curse?"

Famous told her a short version of the story and that it was much like when they went into the map. She placed them around her and said the words, but she had also used them as a light when she was trapped and used them to get out of the room. "Angelica said they are everchanging. I am still trying to get a grip on what that actually means."

"It's kind of like the map. It changes for the situation. If anyone ever says they have it all figured out, they are fooling themselves or lying. Here's the thing, I believe if we come up with the spell, we are as good as there."

"You know, I could call Jonathon." Famous said it like the thought just suddenly occurred to her. "He figured out the spell when I lifted the curse to free the princess."

Destiny didn't say anything. She stood up and walked to the table. She set the book on the table with her map. "Maybe we just hold our map and charm and say, 'Take me to my destination.'" Destiny was looking down at her map. She looked at the destination. "I hadn't really thought about it, but what do you suppose we will find at this destination?" She pointed at the dot on the map.

"That's the forest where Jeremiah lives," Famous answered.

"So, Jeremiah has the book?"

"That can't be right, unless—"

Destiny broke in, "Unless he faked it to get you going in the right direction."

"Do you think? No, he was knocked out."

"Was he? Are you absolutely positive? Did you ever see the book? Maybe this is all about me and you getting your charm. What if we have to break the curse of the monster in the forest together? I mean, now that I think of it, Mawmaw sending me because I'm the only one able to go? I conveniently don't have my passport because we left out in the middle of the night through a tunnel." Destiny was fired up, rambling on. "Think about it, Famous. Sending me? There had to be a reason. I'm practically the misfit of the family. This all had to be planned! Even our meeting at the bus stop. They knew I would talk to you."

"But why? Why not just tell us to go to Iceland and get my charm to break the curse?"

"Did they tell you to go get all the amulets to break the curse? No. You have to follow your mother's journal. It's as much about the journey as it is the destination."

Famous thought about it for a minute, "If that's the case, what do we do now?"

"We create a spell. I bet that's part of it. The page with the spell is blank. What if it wasn't originally blank? Let's just create a spell."

"I don't know, Destiny. I don't want to be trapped ever again. That was horrible. What if we end up trapped in space or something?"

"Don't be ridiculous, Famous. I've been reading these spells. We got this!"

CHAPTER THIRTY-THREE

A STRANGE APPARITION

Famous and Destiny went to work on writing a spell. They looked at other spells in the book to try to come up with the perfect wording. They broke down the riddle believed to be from a wizard's journal.

"You know, it's always about learning so this isn't surprising if you think about it. They have always tried to hide stuff from me. I ask questions and they give me nonsense answers about rules. Like when you came to Mawmaw's house, they kept telling me to be quiet when I tried to tell you stuff. And here we are!"

Time was getting away from them and the minutes ticked by nearing checkout time. Famous read and reread what they had written. "I seriously hope this works because bad things can happen Destiny—really, really, really bad things."

"Oh, trust me I know. My mom has been warning me about using magic practically every minute of my life. She has told me some scary stories to discourage me from trying spells. But I'm feeling confident so all that's left is to do it. At least we're together, right? You are not alone, Famous. I am all in. We got this."

It was touching like Famous had found a long-lost sister. "Yeah, you're right. We got this!" It felt empowering and unnerving at the same time. Famous knew there really wasn't much of an alternative. She knew she would never leave Destiny in a strange country without a passport. She didn't want to ask Darla to send it and wait around for it. Plus, who knows if it would even get to them.

"I guess it's, do-or-die time. First I want to show you a picture of Jeremiah's cottage I took with my phone. That's where we want to end up so I want you to be able to visualize it. We will put on our backpacks and hold hands with the pic on the phone or one of our maps. I don't know. But also hold our charms and the amulets in the other hand. We can't set them down or we may end up leaving them behind."

Destiny could tell Famous was nervous by the way she was talking so fast. They practiced several scenarios with the phone, their maps, and the amulets. They struggled with every scenario.

"Why is this so hard?" Destiny asked with frustration.

Famous read their spell one more time and then a thought occurred to her. "What if we make this easier? This spell seems confusing. I'm nervous we will jumble the words. Why don't we just visualize the book and chant take us to the *Book of Wisdom*?"

Famous put on her backpack and handed Destiny hers. She held her crystal with her map in one hand. She held out her other hand with the amulets. "Take my hand Destiny. We will hold the amulets between our hands and just go. Close your eyes and repeat after me."

Destiny placed her hand on the amulets in Famous's hand and gently squeezed her hand and smiled. "Ready when you are."

They closed their eyes and felt heat like they had never felt before coming from the amulets sandwiched between their hands.

"On our map there is a dot, take us now to that spot," Famous chanted. Destiny joined in and they chanted the words, repeating them over and over. They felt a strange sensation—a sort of vibration and a massive jolt. The ground seemed to disappear under their feet, and they began to fall into darkness.

Famous clung to Destiny's hand so hard she thought it might break. They were falling and falling. Famous screamed to Destiny, "Picture it in your mind and repeat the words with me." They continued to fall and chanted for what seemed like an eternity. They landed suddenly with a thud.

Destiny opened her eyes. It was dark. "Famous?" she called out. No answer. She called out again, "Famous?" She felt around the ground. Her heart was pounding. She screamed her name and started to cry.

Famous shook Destiny. "Wake up, Destiny. Please wake up." She pleaded for her to wake up until Destiny finally opened her eyes. Destiny realized she had only dreamt she was alone in the dark. The ground was cold and wet.

Are you okay?" Famous asked.

Destiny sat up. "I think so. You? Wait, where are we?"

Famous stood up. I was still early morning. The sun had barely begun to rise. Famous looked at her watch realizing it was on Icelandic time, but she was not. The air felt warmer and the trees gently swayed with the breeze. "I think we're in the forest." She heard a rustling behind them. Her head jerked back to look, but she didn't see anything. "Give me your hand, Destiny. I'll help you up."

Destiny grunted as she stood up. "That kind of sucked."

"Yes it did." Famous picked up the amulets one by one and shoved them into her pocket. She heard another noise behind them. "Let's get out of here."

A sound of something running toward them reminded Famous of her nightmare. They began running. Famous was trying to get her bearings and figure out where exactly they might be in the forest. Nothing looked familiar. She could hear her heart thumping in her ears. She looked back to see Destiny was right on her heels. Destiny's foot hit a root. She flew forward, tumbled into Famous, and they rolled down a steep hill.

Famous tumbled onto the edge of the stream at the bottom of the ravine. Destiny landed on top of her.

Both girls lay on the wet ground for a moment, catching their breath. "Doesn't this day just keep getting more and more interesting?" Famous asked sarcastically. She got up and her shoes made a squishing noise as she trudged away from the water.

"Any clues on where we are yet?" Destiny asked as she got up and followed Famous. "I think we need to find a place to dry out. Thank goodness this wasn't the deep end of the pool." The girls laughed and she inspected their backpacks and bodies.

The girls sloshed along next to the stream hoping they were heading in the right direction. Famous heard a voice yelling in the distance. She grabbed Destiny's arm. "Did you hear that?" She held her finger to her lips, "Shh! Listen." A man's voice called out again.

Destiny's eyes got really big. "Can you tell what they are saying?" she hissed.

"Kind of sounds like my name," Famous replied. They scrambled behind a bush. "But no one knows we're here. I mean, how could they?" Destiny gave her a look.

They heard the voice again. "Do you recognize the voice, Famous?" Famous shrugged.

They stood there listening for the voice, barely even taking a breath. Birds chirped. Rustling from a squirrel startled them. They heard the trickling water sound of the stream but no voice.

Destiny tip-toed out into the open to look around. "C'mon," she whispered to Famous and tugged her jacket.

Famous stood her ground and she pulled out her map. She was happy to see the contents of her backpack had not gotten wet. Destiny stepped back to watch it unfold. The lines on the map showed them going in circles, then zigzag, then more circles. "What's up with that?" she asked.

"Hold on," Destiny said as she took her map out. The path on hers wasn't visible except a small line toward the edge that went completely off the map. What the…?"

Famous pulled out her crystal, then closed and opened her map again. This time asking for direction to the *Book of Wisdom*. A spot with a golden glow appeared on the map. "It doesn't look far from here. Do you think the map is all wonky because of the magic traveling?"

Destiny stared at the map. "Maybe. Like I've told you before, these maps will drive you mad."

"Then why even give them to us? If they aren't helpful it's… ugh, I don't know." Famous was frustrated.

"That's just one of the million reasons I get so aggravated. My theory is that they feel like you won't appreciate the gifts you're given, even like special abilities, unless you see the bad side or what can happen if you're not careful."

"So, you think they want bad to happen?"

"No, it's not like that. It's more like they want you to learn about all the possible outcomes through experience."

A loud growl came from behind them. They quickly turned around to see a wolf staring at them, baring it's teeth and growling menacingly.

Backing up into the bushes, they squished together. They stared in horror. Suddenly, a strange apparition seemed to push the wolf away. The wolf turned and began running away whining. They couldn't believe their eyes.

"What was that?" Destiny breathed.

"The monster in the forest?" Famous answeredly uncertainly. She was terrified and thought it best to get out of there. She reached for Destiny's hand and they took off running.

The girls ran wildly for a solid ten minutes. They ran without even realizing the path they were taking—the very path the map had indicated they'd take, zigzags and all.

Stopping, Destiny was bent over with her hands on her knees breathing heavily. Destiny's words came out between breaths. "If that was the monster in the forest, why did it save us?"

"I don't know." Famous answered. She took a deep breath, trying to slow her breathing. A floral scent filled her lungs. She recognized the scent of a fire burning and something baking. "I think I know where we are!" Famous sounded almost giddy as she took off in the direction of the sweet aroma. "Follow me!"

"Wait!" Destiny yelled. "Hold on a sec!" She ran to catch up to Famous. "I've been thinking I should tell you something."

Destiny's voice had sounded unusual. So unusual, it had stopped Famous dead in her tracks.

CHAPTER THIRTY-FOUR

THE TALE OF KERSPIOUS

"What do you know about the monster in the forest?" Destiny asked with trepidation. "Like when you were here before, did it scare you or was it trying to… I don't know."

"What do you know that you're not telling me?" Famous asked, eyeing Destiny with suspicion.

Destiny fidgeted trying to think of what she should or should not tell her. She was reminded of what her grandmother said about the danger of telling her.

"Destiny!" Famous was getting annoyed. "If you know something, you have to tell me!"

"Okay, just tell me what you know first."

Famous thought for half a second before answering. "I don't know anything about the monster in the forest. Before today I was fairly sure it was only a figment of someone's imagination, or maybe a bear. What do you know?"

Destiny was facing away from Famous when they heard the crack of a twig and footsteps behind them. They both turned to see Jeremiah standing in the clearing. "You two girls must be starving," he said with a huge grin.

Destiny's face lit up. "Grandpa, it's so good to see you!" She ran to him leaving Famous standing with a shocked look on her face.

"Grandpa?" Famous was confused. "I didn't know Jeremiah was your Grandpa. Wait… is he my Grandpa, too?"

Jeremiah put his arm around both girls, "We have a lot to talk about, huh, Destiny?"

"Yeah, I guess we do," she replied.

The three of them walked out into the clearing. They could see the archway made of bushes that Famous remembered lead to a cobblestone path, which led to Jeremiah's little cottage. She thought back to her time in this cottage—back in the beginning before it all had really begun.

Once inside the little cottage, Jeremiah went to work setting the table for lunch. Famous sat next to Destiny wondering if any of this made sense. "I don't understand," she said. "Will one of you please explain this to me?"

Jeremiah ignored her while he filled the plates one by one with what looked like hot roast beef sandwiches smothered in brown gravy. He placed them on the table. Then, after filling glasses with lemonade, he sat down with the girls. Famous gave him a questioning look.

"Patience, my child," he said. "It will all be clear soon enough. Let's enjoy our lunch."

"I have like a million questions!" Famous was bursting. "Destiny, when we looked at the picture in the hallway, you said your Grandpa died when you were young."

"Yes, I did. Our mom's dad died when I was young," Destiny answered before shoveling food in her mouth.

"So, Jeremiah is your dad's dad?"

Destiny nodded as she continued to chew.

Jeremiah told Famous to eat and she took a bite. She sat there reeling, trying to understand what was going on. If he was Destiny's grandfather, then he must be her grandfather. But how can that be? It was her mother's journals that brought her here in the first place and they never mentioned Jeremiah was of any relation to her. None of it made sense.

Jeremiah got up from the table and walked out of the room. Famous watched him, confused. "Destiny?" Destiny didn't have time to say anything before Jeremiah reappeared in the doorway. He had an exceptionally large thick, book. Famous could see that it was the *Book of Wisdom*. He set it on the edge of the table.

"This book contains all the answers you could ever want—and maybe some you don't. Now, will you eat your lunch? You can look at it afterward."

Famous stared at the book as she cleaned her plate. Destiny had spent the lunch telling Jeremiah all about their trip. She told him about the lava tunnels, the crystal, and even transporting from Iceland.

After lunch, Famous thanked Jeremiah for the meal. She kept eyeing the book, wondering when she'd be able to steal it away to read somewhere on her own.

Jeremiah noticed her staring at it. "Would you prefer if I told you the story or do you want to read it for yourself?" he inquired.

"Oh, let him tell you the story. He's amazing at telling stories," raved Destiny.

"Either way. I just need to know," Famous answered.

Jeremiah ushered the girls into the little living room. He stoked the fire and began the tale.

"It all began many, many years ago, long before you were born. You know about the princess. Well, the evil witch that cast the spell on her had stolen the seven amulets of the daughters of Kerspious. He was believed to be a Celtic king—a wizard or godlike being, as it's told in the old fables. His wife had died of a horrible disease shortly after the birth of their seventh daughter. Each of the daughters carried one of the amulets that had belonged to his wife's family. Together, they would have been more powerful than ever imaginable. But they were young and did not understand their power. The day the amulets were stolen, the seven sisters disappeared. The king was devastated.

"Over several years, their father never stopped searching for them. He had attempted to use his magic but it yielded no results. He even hired the greatest hunters in all the land, but it was all to no avail. He offered a reward to anyone who could help find his daughters.

"Years and years passed. A young, orphaned boy whose family had been killed by fire brought him the *Book of Wisdom*. Kerspious read the book and learned that a witch had cast a spell on his daughters tricking them into giving her the amulets and then used their own amulets to turn them into stone."

The girls were sitting by the fire hanging onto his every word when he paused. "Let me get you two some cookies," he said with a smile. The girls groaned and protested, but Jeremiah got up and went to the kitchen to retrieve the plate of cookies.

"Grandpa," Destiny growled. "He always does this when he's telling a story." She rolled her eyes.

Jeremiah came back in with cookies in hand. "Stories are better with cookies," he professed. "Anyway, let's see. Where was I?"

"The witch turned them into stone," Famous impatiently reminded him.

"Ah, yes. Now I remember." He sat back and continued his to tell the story. "Kerspious was angered by what he had read. He vowed that she would pay for her misdeeds. He asked his apprentice to bring the young boy back to see him so he could give him his reward.

"When the young boy returned, Kerspious demanded to know where he had gotten the book. He told him that it had belonged to his family. The boy grandmother said it was a magical storybook that can tell you the answers you seek. It was all he had left of his family.

"Kerspious realized the boy must have come from a magical family. He figured he could use the boy's magic to seek vengeance on the evil witch. The king told him that as his reward, the boy would live in his castle as his son. He would become the heir to all of his riches."

Famous was enjoying the story but was growing increasingly impatient for answers. "Jeremiah," she said, "this is a great story and all, but I don't see what this has to do with our current situation."

Jeremiah gave her a look that hushed her. "I'm getting there," he assured her. "Okay, so as I was saying, the boy had been living on scraps off the street so of course he accepted his reward. He was delighted to have a home and food in his belly. Kerspious learned this boy was called Shamus and taught him about magic. They read the *Book of Wisdom* together every evening.

"Over time, as he bonded with Shamus, the pain of losing his wife daughters lessened. Kerspious began to feel joy in his life again. His thoughts of vengeance disappeared. The *Book of Wisdom* had been placed in an old trunk and replaced with books of fairy tales. But I've gotten ahead of myself. We need to go back farther."

With much protestation from the girls, Jeremiah stood up and stoked the fire, got himself a drink of water, and sat back down to continue his tale.

CHAPTER THIRTY-FIVE

THE APPRENTICE

"Before Shamus had come into Kerspious's life, he had had an apprentice. This apprentice came to him to learn about magic. Unknown to Kerspious, he had been sent by a family of witches to learn all of Kerspious's secrets.

"Time passed and Kerspious married. This marked a turning point for the apprentice. It was after the king's marriage that the apprentice began to notice he was treated less and less an apprentice, and more and more a servant. Kerspious spent his days with his wife and children. He told the apprentice his life was different, so he didn't need to practice magic anymore. The lessons ended.

"The apprentice went home to the witches. While he had been gone, his family had learned of the great power of the seven amulets and believed Kerspious's wife had them. They cast a spell of sickness upon Kerspious wife and ordered the apprentice to return to the king.

"Reluctantly, the apprentice returned and begged the king to allow him to stay, telling him he'd do whatever he needed him to do. Kerspious allowed him to stay to care for his wife because her illness continued to worsen. He told the apprentice he had to leave to seek help from her family, and while he was gone, the apprentice was to continue caring for her.

"Kerspious traveled far to the kingdom of his wife's family. Once there, her mother gave him the seven amulets. She told him they had more power than any potion and would cure her. He thanked his mother-in-law and rushed home.

"Kerspious arrived home to find her on her death bed. Kerspious put the amulets in her hand and pleaded for her to use them to get well. Unfortunately, he had grown too weak to use her magic. She died that night.

"The grief of losing his wife was unbearable, but he knew he had to be strong for his daughters. He locked the amulets away and didn't mention them to anyone for years. After some time, the apprentice pressured Kerspious to begin with his teachings again."

Jeremiah stood and stretched. "Maybe we should take a break," he teased. Destiny protested so strongly he sat back down. "Okay, okay, I'll continue," he chuckled. "So the apprentice began to pressure Kerspious to continue with his lessons. He finally agreed and began teaching both him and his daughters about magic. A day came when he gave each of his daughters one of the amulets, but the apprentice did not receive one.

"Seeing the amulets truly existed, the apprentice sent word to his family. Not long after, the seven daughters vanished along with the amulets. The apprentice remained with Kerspious, vowing to help him find his daughters. What Kerspious didn't know was the apprentice's vow was just to keep up appearances because it was he who had the amulets and his family who had made the daughters disappear.

"After Shamus came along, the apprentice became jealous. He watched and learned about the *Book of Wisdom*. One day he watched as Kerspious put it in an old chest.

"Days, weeks, and months passed, and the apprentice watched the relationship grow between Shamus and Kerspious. One day, when Kerspious took Shamus on a hunting excursion, the apprentice snuck into the king's room. He took the *Book of Wisdom* and ran away to join his family."

CHAPTER THIRTY-SIX

THE SON NAMED JEREMIAH

Jeremiah got up and added wood to the fire. He grabbed himself and the girls another drink, then continued his story.

"Kerspious raised Shamus to be a man. The *Book of Wisdom* and the amulets had been long forgotten until the day Kerspious had taken ill from old age. He told Shamus of the amulets and asked Shamus to seek answers from the *Book of Wisdom*. It was only then that they realized the book was gone. They had no way of knowing how long it had been missing.

"On his death bed, he told Shamus to find a wife, raise a family, and forget about magic because it had only brought evil into his life. It was only after he and Shamus had put the book away and stopped practicing magic that his life had really begun. Shamus spent the days caring for his father until old age finally took him away.

"Shamus grieved for the father that took him off the streets and showed him kindness. He became angry that his father had been taken from him when he could have been saved if only they had the book. The book belonged to him and, although he planned to honor his father's dying wishes, he wanted it back. So after burying his father, he set out to find it.

"Shamus was unsuccessful in finding the *Book of Wisdom*. He had searched for years until meeting a woman in a small village. She was an innkeeper's daughter named Ganesa. He married her and returned home to Kerspious's castle. Together, they had a son who was named Jeremiah."

Famous bolted upright. "Wait, what? Did you say Shamus had a son named Jeremiah?"

"Yes, I did say that."

"So, we are getting closer to this century!" she exclaimed. Destiny elbowed her and told her to be quiet.

"Now Destiny," Jeremiah chided, "you have been part of this for a long time. You are not being fair to Famous. Famous, in order for you to understand today, you needed to know what happened back then.

"My childhood began pretty normal until one day, I accidently turned a school bully into a frog. That was the day I learned I came from a line of wizards. I really didn't mean to do it. I merely wished he were a frog and, just like that, he was. That was a challenging year for my parents." The girls giggled and he continued, "My father eventually had to tell me the story of the *Book of Wisdom* and about his great-grandfather being a wizard. That meant my great, great-grandfather was a wizard. Next thing you know I was trying all kinds of magic.

"My father did all he could to keep me from practicing magic. He warned me of all the evils and told me everything he could about Kerspious and how it affected his life.

"Eventually, I grew up and married. I had twin sons—your fathers."

Famous's eyes grew large and she said, "Whoa, whoa, whoa. You're telling me our mothers were twin sisters and our fathers were twin brothers? What kind of crazy is this family?" She looked at Jeremiah and then to Destiny. "Did you know this the whole time?"

"No. Well, not all of it. Especially that last part," Destiny said with shock. "I mean, I knew your mom and my mom were twins, but the twin dads thing… that's definitely new information. I thought the witch—"

"Don't get ahead of the story, Destiny," Jeremiah interrupted.

Famous's eyes grew larger. "You mean there's more?"

"Have we gotten to the monster?" he asked.

Famous could not believe this was real. Who would believe that it was?

"Shall I continue?"Jeremiah asked.

Destiny glared at Famous. "Yes, do go on please, Grandpa."

Famous nodded. "Yes, we've come this far. I doubt anything else could possibly shock me anymore."

Jeremiah winked at her and said, "Hold on to that thought, Famous." He continued his story.

"Well, this whole time the apprentice and his family were casting some pretty evil curses. And in case you haven't figured it out after hearing of the curse on the princess, that means Daniel is a descendant of the apprentice. Anyway, somewhere along the line they put a curse on my two sons—that they would be stuck here in the forest forever after each of their first children were conceived. They'd be stuck kind of between worlds. You two were born within months of each other and once you were born, your fathers had merely vanished.

"This is the reason I live here in the forest. Because my two sons—your fathers—are essentially the monster in the forest. The times you felt like they were following you to harm you, they were only protecting you.

"Now, I knew that Famous's mother had stolen the *Book of Wisdom*. I found it and got a chance to read a little before she placed it in the public library for safe keeping. She also stole the amulets and hid them in various locations. Only she knew where the amulets were located.

"You know the rest of the story. All of this—getting your crystal, you two bonding—has all happened so we can break the curse to set your fathers free and bring them back to us."

Finally it all made sense. Famous understood, but still felt like she was living in an episode of "The Twlight Zone."

"I must admit that over the past month or two, I have experienced things that no sane person would ever believe. I have embraced the possibility that I have fully lost my mind and am locked in a world of delusions. I know I'm not crazy, but this is just too much to take in. I need a minute." Famous thought about everything for a moment. "Are you saying my father is still alive?"

"In a matter of speaking, yes," Jeremiah answered. "Both of your fathers are still alive. At least, as far as I know."

"So what's next?" Famous asked.

Destiny grabbed Famous by the hand. They looked each other in the eyes. "I guess the only thing to do is lift the curse and meet our dads," Destiny said.

Famous and Destiny began preparations to break the curse. They began to read about it in the *Book of Wisdom*. As they were reading, Jeremiah had gone to bed and Destiny had drifted off to sleep. The furry little creatures had come out and were curled up on Famous's lap.

Famous stopped reading for a moment to stretch her legs and cover Destiny with a blanket. She looked around the room thinking about her life and how it had finally come full circle. She thought about her mom. She remembered reading her journals and wondered if her mom had known all before she died. Did she know the story before she started writing her journals—the very journals that led Famous to find herself?

Famous grabbed a big squishy pillow and warm fuzzy blanket. She closed the *Book of Wisdom* and lay down by the fire thinking about her mom. Her eyes grew heavy. She could no longer keep them open and she fell asleep.

CHAPTER THIRTY-SEVEN

A Hole In The Universe

There is nothing better than waking up to the smell of bacon. Clanking noises from the kitchen had woke her, and Famous slowly opened her eyes. She looked around the room and saw Destiny was still fast asleep on the couch. She reached over and tugged on her sleeve. "Hey Des, are you still sleeping?"

"Hmm?" Destiny answered as she stretched.

"Okay, you two sleepy heads. It's time for breakfast," Jeremiah called from the kitchen.

The girls slowly made their way to the table. The table had been set and there were piles of some kind of a scramble on each of their plates. A large plate with bacon and toast sat in the center of the table.

Jeremiah whistled while he poured coffee and juice for each of them. "Today is going to be a big day. It's best starting it off right," he said with a smile.

Famous sipped her coffee and watched Destiny shovel food in her mouth like she hadn't eaten in days. She picked at her own breakfast, taking small bites. "You know, last night I read about the curse and even the spell to break the curse," Famous mentioned. "It's a pretty simple spell."

Jeremiah looked up from his breakfast. "I guess that is true, but it was a lot of work to get to this point. Both of you had to come here with your charms and the seven amulets together. With you two girls living in different worlds, so to speak, that was tricky."

Destiny smiled. "It was probably a logistical nightmare." Famous agreed.

After cleaning up from breakfast, Famous, Destiny, and Jeremiah began getting ready to journey deeper into the forest. Suddenly, a thought occurred to Famous. "What about Daniel?" she asked.

"Don't worry about Daniel," replied Jeremiah. "Your grandmother and Darla have taken care of him for the time being."

They began their trek through the Forest— Destiny and Famous together and Jeremiah following a little ways behind. Famous told Destiny what she had read the night before. They needed to be exactly where they had landed the day before when they did the spell.

Fortunately for them, Jeremiah had known this. He had planned on meeting them there when they landed, but he was running late—or they were earlier than he had anticipated. It was Jeremiah they had heard him running toward them when they got scared and ran away.

Once they reached the spot, Famous and Destiny set out the amulets in a circle around them. They faced each other and held hands. Destiny's medallion was sandwiched between her right and Famous's left hand. Famous's crystal was sandwiched between her right and Destiny's left hand. They began chanting some words that, to most, would sound like nonsense. Heat vibrated through them as they chanted. The light from the amulets was blinding. The ground shook. When describing what had happened to her grandmother, Famous would later say it felt like a hole in the universe had opened and their fathers fell from the sky.

The girls spent several days with Jeremiah and their fathers. They told the men all that had happened while they were away. Their fathers returned home, but the girls did not join them. Jeremiah had told Famous and Destiny that they had to find a safe place for the *Book of Wisdom* and the amulets. But that's another story.